BITS
AND
PIECES

For
Sweet Kathryn *

April 16th 2015

All The Best!

Phil C

BITS
AND
PIECES

A Potpourri of Prose and Poetry

Phillip L. Pendergast

Phillip L. Pendergast

Riverhaven Books
www.RiverhavenBooks.com

* may your future travels be—
SWARM ~~FREE~~ FREE!

Published in the United States by Riverhaven Books,
www.RiverhavenBooks.com

ISBN: 978-1-937588-29-8

Cover photo by Phillip L. Pendergast

Front cover design and layout by
Bay State Color, Hanover, Massachusetts

Back cover and interior layout by
Stephanie Blackman, Whitman, Massachusetts

Printed in the United States of America
by Country Press, Lakeville, Massachusetts

DEDICATION

*For my wife, Gail,
with my love and gratitude for your loyalty, support,
and love for almost fifty years.*

You are one amazing wife and mom!

In loving memory of my two exceptional parents:

*Richard Leo Pendergast
April 21st, 1913-May 15th, 2000*

*Claudia Macbeth Pendergast
August 21st, 1915-December 10th, 2001*

Table of Contents

BITS AND PIECES

A person's life is made up of many bits and pieces. Bits and pieces of minutes, hours, days, weeks, months and years. Bits and pieces of hopes, dreams and goals. Bits and pieces of challenges and choices. All these bits and pieces work together to form our Life Puzzle.

When I was just a young boy, I figured that when I grew up I would: 1. Graduate high school; 2. Go to college; 3. Secure a well-paying job; 4. Get married; and 5. Have four children (boy, girl, boy, girl…each two years apart!)

Over time, I planned to work hard and excel at whatever career I had chosen. Then I would buy a nice oceanfront house on Cape Cod and live a long, comfortable life! Hmmm…

Over the years, I took my bits and pieces and put together my Life Puzzle. Now that I am in my third act, I stepped back to take a good look at my puzzle. This sure didn't turn out the way I had so naively planned! I saw that there were some places where my pieces fit together perfectly and some of my goals were realized. However, there were far more places (or spaces) where my life had taken turns that I had never anticipated. Some of these puzzle pieces had formed to create blessings and joy. But, I had to admit, that there were places where some of my decisions and actions had affected others in ways that were not always good.

However, I was grateful to see that there were some areas where my pieces had fit in nicely and brought some harmony and comfort. I had never really thought about just how important each tiny little piece was and how it contributed to the whole picture. Not one single piece was insignificant. Each had an important role to play.

Upon further reflection, I decided to look over my Life Puzzle again. I felt so happy, humble, and grateful for all that I had been given. I saw that there were still spaces in my puzzle that had not been filled in completely. I looked at the remaining pieces. I knew that I would always be working on my Life Puzzle as long as I lived. I resolved to use my remaining life as effectively as possible. When my time on earth ends, God will call me home, fill in any remaining pieces, and explain to me the mosaic that is my Life Puzzle.

****

1

ARTHUR ITIS

My name is Arthur Itis and I'm a jolly bloke.
But, if I come to visit you, it will not be a joke.
Not being snobby is one of my good points.
That's why you often find me in so many of your joints.

I love to set up residence in your lower back.
And often that's the place that I first attack.
I'm not a picky being. Any back is fine.
From there I often relocate to your upper spine.

Everybody hates me. They consider me a pain.
Some folks even say I'm driving them insane.
Many times you'll find me in shoulders, hips, and knees.
Fact is I reside anywhere I please.

I really get around, as you can plainly see.
And many older ladies have been found in bed with me.
Now if you haven't met me, don't go whine and pout.
It's just a matter of time until I check YOU out!

****

STRANGE HAPPENINGS AT AMY'S HOUSE

I'd like to share with you a true story that occurred about thirty years ago when I first started to sell real estate as my second career.

One bright October day when I was on "up time" (answering the phone), I got a call from a man who wanted me to come out immediately to list his house for sale. So I drove to the neighboring town with my listing forms, marketing tools, and great expectations.

As I drove up to the house, I was disappointed to see how dilapidated and run-down it looked. The property was an antique, weather-beaten Cape Cod-style home set back from the road. Some of the shutters were missing, others were hanging off, and it was obvious that the place had not been painted in many years. The wood was so dry and rotted that many of the nails were actually popping out of the clapboards. There was a detached two-car garage off to the left and some crumbling outbuildings were visible beyond the house. Lastly, the lawn had virtually turned into a large hay field.

I opened the broken, wooden screen door and knocked on the entry door. Eventually the door opened and I was greeted by an unkempt man with wild eyes, shaggy, wiry hair, and a hint of body odor. He appeared to be 30-40 years old, but it was hard to be certain. He introduced himself as Ralph and said, "Come on in." He introduced me to his mother, a short, stooped woman dressed all in black, who sat at the kitchen table and regarded me with an unfriendly expression and suspicious eyes.

I was offered a cup of coffee that I declined since the table was covered with an oilskin cloth that was filthy and looked like it had never been cleaned. Ralph said, "I might as well tell you right off that this house is haunted. This place has been on and off the market for years and you are the third broker."

I asked Ralph if he had actually seen anything unusual in the house such as a ghost. He replied that they had had an exorcist out to the house and were told that there was "...a ghost in every room." He went on to say that he had "...seen an Indian, a pirate, and a little girl named Amy..." who regularly appeared. He went on to state that he "...had a lonely life..." and that his "...best friend..." was this Amy, who had

3

been murdered in the house about 150 years ago, when she was seven years old. He told me that they played and colored together and that he even had a picture that he had drawn of Amy. Before I left, he handed me a picture of a young girl he had drawn with what appeared to have been crayons. As I rode back to my office, I wondered just what I had gotten myself into.

A few days later, when a fellow broker stopped in for a key, I told him about my new listing. He informed me that he was the second broker and that Ralph and his mother were "really crazy." He suggested that I watch my back whenever I went out there. Whenever he had gone out to the house, he had told his associate to "Call the cops if I'm not back within two hours." At this point, I was really wishing that I hadn't gotten involved with these clients. However, the house was listed and it was too late now.

The following day I drove out to the house to put up our "For Sale" signs, measure the rooms, and take black-and-white Polaroid pictures. While I was there, Ralph wanted to show me the out-building where his father had slaughtered the turkeys. Apparently, at one time his father had raised turkeys to sell. I felt uncomfortable walking ahead of him when it flashed through my mind that I had once been called a turkey. I dropped back and let Ralph lead.

After viewing the old turkey shed inside and out, we started to walk through the hay, back to the house. Ralph stopped abruptly and pointed out the cover of what at one time had been an old well. It had since been converted to a cesspool since there was no town sewage.

"Phillip, do you know what's at the bottom of that cesspool?" he asked.

I said, "I have no idea."

Ralph went on to say, "There's a skeleton down there, Phillip. That's what I call being permanently shit-faced."

I couldn't think of a reply and we walked in silence back to his house. Before I left, Ralph asked if he could have one of the four Polaroid's I had taken.

Within minutes of returning to my office, the phone rang. It was Ralph. "Phillip, have you got your pictures there? Your camera saw something it wasn't supposed to see."

I asked him what he was talking about. He proceeded to tell me that Amy's face was looking out of a first-floor window. I checked my three photos, but couldn't find any Amy. "Well, she's definitely in my picture." he insisted. I told him that I would look with a magnifying glass when I had more time.

Later that week we all went on our weekly house tours to view our new listings. I told everyone that I had a special treat for them. Needless to say, it was quite entertaining as Ralph led us through the house, including the attic, garage, and outbuildings. Everyone agreed that Ralph was mentally unbalanced. About the house being haunted? Well, maybe there was some paranormal activity going on out there. We all agreed that we had to disclose that the owner stated that the place was haunted.*

One of our brokers hadn't made the house tour. So I went back the next day so she could see the property. She thought that Ralph was "Certifiable" and that any noise that he had heard in the attic was just some rats or mice scampering around.

The next day, Ralph called to ask what the brokers had thought of the listed price and also what we thought about the ghost. I told him that we all thought the price was realistic. However, I also told him that one of the brokers thought that there weren't any ghosts and that what he heard was just some mice in the attic. Ralph became very angry and said, "I'd like to lock her up in that attic some night and see what she has to say the next day."

A few days later, Ralph called and told me to come down immediately and collect my signs. He stated that the ghosts were angry

5

and did not want the house sold. He added that all the ghosts were acting up because it was almost Halloween. He said that, "Last Halloween mother and I had to go and sleep in our car because of loud organ music and increased ghost activity."

The following week, Ralph called again to say that things had quieted down and he wanted to sell again. So I drove out to his house again, put the signs back up, and reactivated the listing in the MLS.

Eventually, we did obtain some excellent buyers for the property. It was a group of pediatricians who wanted to tear the house down and build a professional building on the site. The doctors had heard all about the history of the house and were not interested in meeting with the owners. Therefore, they wanted to purchase the property as is without viewing the inside or having any inspections. They were, indeed, the perfect buyers.

The passing was quickly scheduled because there were no inspections or financing required. The day of the closing arrived, and we all sat in the lawyer's office awaiting the arrival of Ralph and his mother. They were already fifteen minutes late. I started remembering how they had backed out at the last minute on their sale with the first broker. Finally, after another fifteen minutes, they walked in and signed the necessary paperwork. We all shook hands, then Ralph and his mother drove off in their old, black sedan. And so ends this story of one of my first and most memorable real estate transactions.

****

EPILOGUE

Was that house truly haunted? I really don't know. However, I do know that I would have never stayed overnight in that house with or without Ralph and his mother.

Ralph and his mother apparently ended up renting an apartment on the second floor of a two-family in a neighboring town. However, about one month later my office phone rang. It was Ralph. "Phillip, you've got to find us another apartment. The tenants downstairs are driving us crazy and we cannot sleep." We honestly did not have any rental units available at that time, so I gave Ralph the names and numbers of some agents who tended to deal in rentals. That was about thirty years ago and I've never heard from Ralph since.

* Today, Realtors® refer to these as stigmatized houses.

TIME OUT OF MIND

This short story is dedicated to my good friend Russ Card who is a true "Maine-iac" and knows the highways and back roads of Maine like the back of his hand. In his youth he was indeed known as "The Wild Card."

Bang! The beat up old Ford 150 pickup truck hit another pothole as it bumped along the rutted-out country road. The driver, Toby Crocker, was not a happy camper. In fact, he was fuming. He had somehow managed to exit off the main highway too soon. He was now somewhere outside of Madawaska in northern Maine.

At this rate, he was never going to make it home to Bangor within three hours. His wife, Mable, was really going to flip out this time. She was planning a family birthday party for her mom who was just turning eighty. This surprise party had been planned for weeks and it was all Mable had been talking about. She had reminded Toby over and over to be sure to be on time for once.

It seemed that he had a history of wandering in late whenever she had a family gathering. Well, the truth was, Toby couldn't stand family get-togethers. He was just not a "people-person" like Mable. He preferred the simple life. He loved to go hunting or fishing whenever he had the chance. Yup, he considered himself a man's man, a true "Maine-iac," born and bred.

For the past half hour, all Toby had seen was acres and acres of dead corn stalks and some rotted pumpkins. There were no road signs anywhere. He had no idea where the hell he was at this point. To make matters worse, it was now 4:30 and soon it would be dark. With no streetlights, things were not going to go well. To top it off, Toby's night vision had deteriorated over the last few years. He wished Mable were here to do the night driving like she usually did. This day was sure not going well, Toby thought.

Toby had spent the last week up at the family log cabin on the lake. He had really enjoyed the chance to meet up with his brothers for some good fishing and hunting. The brothers had left yesterday to head back to New York; Toby had volunteered to stay and close up the cabin for the winter. He had drained the pipes, stacked the firewood, and boarded up some of the windows. After this, he was a little tired so he lay down on the couch to finish that James Patterson paperback he was reading. He quickly fell asleep and awoke about an hour later. Realizing he was behind schedule, he quickly packed his bags, locked the cabin, threw his duffel into the back of his truck, and headed for Bangor.

Within the last ten minutes, it had become increasingly dark. Even the crescent moon was obscured by some low-hanging clouds. Toby now had to slow down to not much more than a crawl. The fact that his night vision had deteriorated added to his distress. He started to feel uncomfortable and ill at ease. He didn't really like driving out of his comfort zone at night. Well, at least it wasn't pouring rain. Then he would have had to pull over and wait it out.

After another few miles, he came to a fork in the road. Since there were no posted signs, he had to make a decision. He remembered that old saying, "Go right and you won't be wrong." Well, he did go right--- and he was wrong! After a few miles, the road got even rougher and he felt that now that he was on some abandoned logging road. "Oh, great. Just great," he fumed. Just where the heck was he anyway? Now, Toby was starting to become a little panicked. He didn't like losing control and now he had. He just prayed that soon he would come to some kind of sign leading to a main road. He knew now that he was never going to make it back to Bangor in time for the party.

He decided to pull over a minute and call Mable on his cell phone. Now he was glad that he had listened to her. She was always reminding him to take his cell with him. Now he was glad he did. He reached into his right jacket pocket where he always kept it. It wasn't there! Then, with a sinking feeling, he remembered that, in his haste, he'd left it on the kitchen table. Damn it. Now he was running about two hours late and he was lost on some God-forsaken logging road somewhere in northern Maine with no cell phone. Just Ducky! Well, at least I have a full tank of gas, he thought. It could be worse…I guess.

A few miles further down the road, he was startled when a blinding light flooded the interior of his truck. Oh, good, he thought. Maybe he could follow this person out of this wilderness. But Toby was amazed to see that this brilliant light shot up into the air and disappeared ahead of him behind the next hill.

"What the hell was THAT?" I must be really losing it, he thought. As he continued along the rutted road, he began to feel increasingly uneasy. He decided to flip on the radio to his favorite country music

8

station. Country music always helped to relax him. However, after a few minutes, the music started to fade out. Then there was a lot of static and some crackling noises and the radio went dead. Toby tried all the other stations but nothing. Brother! What else can possibly go wrong tonight? he thought.

The old Ford continued slowly along the abandoned road. As he rounded the next bend, he saw brilliant blue flashing strobe-type lights over the next ridge. At that precise moment, the truck started losing power and it suddenly stalled out. Toby tried the ignition key several times. Not even a click. Was he going to be stuck out here all night with a stalled truck, no lights and no cell? The hairs on the back of his neck seemed to bristle and for the first time in his forty-two years; Toby Crocker was a truly frightened man. He now checked his Indiglo Timex watch. The lighted dial read 5:33. Then it flashed twice and went blank. "I do NOT believe this! What else can possibly go wrong? This is what I get for falling asleep and leaving late. This mess wouldn't have happened if Mable were here."

Since his truck was dead, Toby decided to get out and hike up the ridge to see what those lights were all about. He grabbed a flashlight and "Betsy", his trusty 12-gauge shotgun. He was a card-carrying NRA member and always wore his official black hat.

Once he reached the summit of the hill, he was stunned at the sight displayed before him. A huge, triangular shaped craft had landed among all the reeds and dried corn stalks. It was a shiny, black metallic color and it seemed to resemble a Stealth Bomber, only much smaller. There appeared to be an observation bubble or window near its nose. It regularly flashed brilliant blue strobe-type lights and it emitted a very high-pitched beeping sound.

Toby covered his ears because they started to hurt due to those high decibel sounds. He had to avert his eyes and look at the ground because the flashing strobe lights were burning his eyes. He was absolutely terrorized, but he couldn't move his feet. It was as if they were glued to the ground. He knew instinctively that he was being somehow observed. He wanted to run as fast as he could and get back to the safety of his truck. Suddenly, he felt something like an electrical current surge through him. Within seconds he fell to the ground, unconscious.

The next sensation Toby experienced was a high-pitched chirping sound. It slowly increased in intensity and sounded almost musical to

9

him. He tried unsuccessfully to open his eyes, but they were stuck shut somehow. Eventually, he became aware of cloudy shapes moving back and forth behind his closed eyelids. Finally, after a lot of effort, he was able to blink his eyes open. At first all he could discern were very bright lights and blurry shapes flitting across his field of vision. After a few more seconds of trying to focus, he was jolted to see a huge set of black compound eyes staring intently at him.

My God, this cannot be real! he thought.

But it was real and the eyes continued to stare at him. Toby began to feel faint and very dizzy and he quickly lost consciousness.

He awoke to find himself lying naked on some kind of table with a metallic sheet placed under him. He felt very cold and he was tingling all over. He now became aware that there were other figures gathered around him. They were very short, maybe four feet tall with huge heads and gigantic eyes. It appeared that there were two holes where their mouths should have been. They all had spindly arms and legs and web-like fingers. They seemed to communicate by making musical beeping and chirping noises. He tried hard to concentrate, think clearly, and organize his thoughts. However, he slowly came to the conclusion that he had probably been drugged somehow. As he became more lucid, he realized that there were four or five beings in this chamber with him. Suddenly, they all started beeping loudly at once as they gathered around him. Of one thing Toby was certain: they were all very excited and seemed to be examining him. He never had the feeling that they wished to harm him.

As Toby continued to slowly regain his senses, he saw that many small tubes had been inserted into his mouth, nostrils and ears. There were also small metallic pads taped across his chest and belly with wires attached. All these wires and tubes appeared to lead to machines with blinking yellow and green lights. Next, Toby felt like he was being slid into some kind of machine similar to CAT scan equipment. He was subjected to loud banging and clanging noises that really hurt his ears. He felt as if his eardrums would surely burst. As soon as he emerged from this machine, the faces around him became very blurry and cloudy again. He knew right away that more drugs had been administered to him. He felt dizzy and quickly lost consciousness again.

When Toby next awoke, he was lying naked on his stomach on the same metallic sheet. Soon he felt some kind of ointment being rubbed onto his back. This cream felt very cool and soothing to him. However, all of a sudden, he felt some kind of very hot objects being arranged on his back and then pressed into his skin. It felt to Toby as if little fires had been set all over his back. At this same time, he felt little electrical shocks where the patches of pain were. The shocks ended with one powerful electrical surge. Toby screamed out in pain and passed out for the third time.

The next thing Toby knew, he awoke to find himself laying in some tall grass and shrubs next to the road and not too far from his truck. He was glad to see that "Betsey" was lying by his side. He felt cold, groggy and very tired. He also ached all over. He got up very slowly and looked over at the ridge where the spacecraft had been. He heard no noise and saw no pulsing strobe lights. He grabbed Betsey and his flashlight and crawled to the top of the ridge. He scanned quickly with his flashlight and saw that the field was empty and the spacecraft was gone. All that appeared to remain was the smell of burned leaves and wood and a strong odor of smoke and what smelled like sulfur.

Toby staggered over to his truck. He got in and sat for a few moments in the driver's seat. Then he put in the key into the ignition and turned it. To his surprise, it started right up. At the same time, his radio came back on in the middle of a country song. He checked his Timex and it was still not working. The time still registered 5:45. Just then, the country song ended and the time was announced on the radio prior to the daily news. It was now 6:30 pm. He had lost forty-five minutes! Now, Toby started wondering exactly what had happened during the time that he could not account for. Slowly, he started to remember parts of his ordeal and he became very frightened. He just wanted to get out of these woods and back to Mabel as fast as possible. The big problem was he was still lost.

Toby sat in the truck for about ten minutes and tried to slow down his racing thoughts. He was well aware that he had been through a very traumatic experience. He also knew that his life was never going to be quite the same again. He finally pulled back onto the rutted road. After a few more minutes of driving, he saw lights in his rear view mirror. Toby's heart started to race again and he gripped the steering wheel with sweaty hands. "No! Please God. Don't have them come back again." But he soon discovered that that the lights were only headlights of an approaching vehicle. Toby flashed his lights off and on and

11

honked his horn.

Within minutes, a Cherokee Jeep pulled up alongside of him. The driver rolled down his window and Toby poked his head out of his window.

A friendly voice from the jeep said, "Hey, Buddy. Need help?"

Toby explained that he was lost and was trying to get home to Bangor.

The older man in the jeep replied, "Well, I guess you ARE lost! You're on an abandoned logging road out in the middle of Stockholm! You're a long way from the Maine highway. But don't worry, young feller. I'm on my way to Bangor myself right now. My wife, Theresa, and I are on our way to visit our granddaughter, Tish, and her family. Just follow me and I'll lead you right out to the highway."

Toby was overjoyed at his good fortune. He followed very closely behind the jeep. No way did he ever want to lose this guy. After about fifteen minutes, Toby found himself on a tarred road with several large, green signs with white arrows pointing the way to the main highway. Toby slowed down and flashed his lights again. The jeep stopped and Toby pulled up alongside of it.

"Thank you very much. I'm very grateful that you came along when you did."

"No problem. Just glad to help out. Just follow those signs out to the highway and you will be all set."

"Thanks again, friend. By the way, what's your name?"

"My name is Russ Card. But a lot of folks around these parts call me 'The Wild Card.' I was kind of a hell-raiser in my younger days."

"Well, as far as I'm concerned, you're my 'Lucky Card,'" Toby replied.

Russ Card laughed, said good-bye, and rolled up his window. Then the jeep took off down the road headed for Bangor.

Toby followed the signs directing him south to Bangor. Eventually he found himself back on the Maine Turnpike heading home at last. However, Toby was not looking forward to the long three-hour drive. He was totally exhausted and he ached all over. He also felt like he now had the flu as he had developed chills and fever. He just wanted to get home, hug Mable, and go right to bed.

Toby had the road to himself as he drove along so he was able to go a little faster than the posted speed limit. As he drove, he began to envision Mable's reception when he finally did arrive home. She would be livid as he was going to be at least two hours late. He felt bad about getting home so late because he was very fond of his mother-in-law (or "Ma" as everyone called her). She was a very loving woman with a great sense of humor. She and Toby were avid Red Sox fans and he and Mable had taken Ma to several games at Fenway Park over the years.

Toby began rehearsing just what he would say to explain his tardiness to Mable and the family. He decided to be completely honest and just tell everyone exactly what happened and as much as he could remember. He figured that no one would believe that he had had an encounter with some aliens. However he felt that they all deserved to hear the truth no matter how bizarre. But he still dreaded to hear what their reaction would be. Mable would be sure to have something sarcastic to say. His two children (Tony, 20, and Nancy, 17) would probably double over laughing and refuse to believe him.

The one person who would be the worst to deal with would be Troy, his know-it-all brother-in-law. Troy was the quintessential New York Yuppie. He was Mable's older brother and he had become a very successful drug rep. Troy always managed to find some way to infer that Toby was basically a blue-collar hick. Troy was actually one of the reasons that Toby tried to avoid the family gatherings on Mable's side of the family. But there would be no way to avoid Troy. He would most definitely be there. As usual, he would be expounding on the global economy, politics, or whatever was currently being discussed by the talking heads on the only channel that he ever watched, Fox News. "Fair and balanced," Troy always reminded Toby.

As soon as Toby pulled into this driveway, the first thing his headlights illuminated was the New York license plate on Troy's Mercedes. He gripped the steering wheel tighter and uttered, "Lord, please give me patience and keep me calm." Toby parked his truck and grabbed one of the duffle bags from the back. He was too tired to try to lug them all in. He walked slowly up to his house and quietly opened the kitchen door. The room was empty. He could see the table and the empty chairs, the dirty dishes and the half-eaten birthday cake. There were some opened presents and some birthday cards set at the edge of the cluttered table. Apparently everyone had finished eating and they were now in the family room. He could hear the sounds of people laughing and a Rod Stewart CD playing. Rod Stewart was one of Ma's favorite singers and she had all his old tapes and new CD's. Toby squared his shoulders, took a deep breath and stepped into the room. All conversation abruptly stopped.

"Well, look who decided to drop by!" Mable said. "How nice of you to make an appearance."

Toby stood still for a few seconds. Then he very slowly and calmly tried to explain about what had happened to him and why he was late. Even as he was speaking, he could tell that his story sounded totally ridiculous. Everyone just stared at him. However he had no idea what they were thinking.

Mable listened patiently and then said, "Well, you know what happened to ME today? Peter Pan stopped in and we flew up to Neverland! But, at least I made it back in time for the party."

Then Troy piped up, "Toby, did you happen to bring one of those alien chicks back with you? I heard they're pretty hot. Is she sitting out in the truck by herself? Go bring her in so she can join the party. I'd really like to have my picture taken with her. Ha, ha, ha."

There was a burst of laughter and Toby felt his face redden with anger and embarrassment. His two children just smiled at each other and rolled their eyes. The few remaining guests quietly sipped their drinks and pretended to be in deep conversation with whoever happened to be sitting next to them.

It was Ma who gently came to his rescue. "Toby, I'm so glad to see you! Never mind those kidders. Sit down right next to me. I have a plate of food right here for you," she said as she patted the couch. "You really don't look well at all, dear. You look like you haven't slept in a week. Have some hot food and you'll feel better."

About an hour later, the last guests departed and Toby was left with just the family. Nancy was on her cell with her current boyfriend. Troy and Tony were playing a video game on the new wide screen TV. Ma had already excused herself and gone to bed as she and Troy were staying overnight.

Once they were alone, Mable sat down next to Toby and gently draped her arm over his shoulder.

"Okay, Toby, please be honest with me and tell me the real reason that you were late."

Toby looked at her wearily and tried to choose his words very carefully. He told Mable the parts of his ordeal that he could actually remember. He explained again about getting a late start and ending up on the abandoned logging road in Stockholm. He described the flashing blue strobe-type lights and the strange looking spacecraft. After that his mind became jumbled and he lost about forty-five minutes. He told her he remembered waking up by the side of the road. He went on to say that he was pretty sure that he had been inside the craft, but everything was very hazy and blurry. He felt that he may have been drugged somehow. Then, sometimes he felt that he had merely dreamed about actually being inside the spacecraft. Of one thing he was sure: he had definitely seen a UFO up close. He felt that he could probably even draw a picture of it. He also remembered the smell of burned wood and sulfur where the spaceship had been after it left. Unfortunately, the more he talked, the angrier Mable seemed to become. Finally, she removed her hand from his shoulder and abruptly jumped up.

"Toby, please don't insult my intelligence any more with this alien, UFO babble. I just cannot believe that you can spin all this stuff. Why not just man up and admit that you stayed longer at the cabin to do a little more fishing with your brothers? I am really tired of your lame excuses every time you wander in late to one of our family gatherings. But THIS story really takes first prize. I'm sleeping on the couch in the family room tonight. See you tomorrow morning. Maybe by that time you will be honest with me and tell me what really happened." Mabel stomped off headed for the bedroom to ready herself for sleep.

Toby dragged himself to his feet and walked slowly to the bedroom. He was far too tired to argue any more with Mabel. In fact he was so tired that it took all his energy to just make it to the bed. He kicked off his shoes and laid down on the king-size bed without even undressing. Within seconds, he fell into a deep, dreamless sleep. He was soon snoring loudly. However this time Mabel wasn't there to jab him in the ribs and tell him he was keeping her awake.

Toby awoke at 7:30 the next morning to the sounds of some birds chirping happily outside his window. The smells of bacon and freshly brewed coffee wafted into the bedroom. Mabel must be making breakfast for Ma, Troy, and the kids he thought.

Toby yawned, stretched and slowly got out of bed. He walked into the bathroom and stripped off his clothes. He let them just fall onto the floor outside the new glassed-in shower. He stepped into the shower and immediately adjusted the water temperature to very hot, the way he liked it. The rushing water felt wonderful on his tired body and he built up a good lather with the soap. He rinsed his chest and then turned his back to the running water. The very second that the cascading water hit his back, he yelled out in agony. His whole back was burning like someone had poured gasoline on it and put a match to it. He jumped out of the shower still screaming and jumping up and down in pain and frustration.

Mabel rushed into the room and found Toby staggering out of the steamy bathroom. She took one look at Toby's back and she yelled out, "Toby, your back. It's covered with deep red markings. It looks almost like there are some hieroglyphic writings inside the shapes. Toby, I really think that you have been branded somehow!"

Later that afternoon found Toby at the clinic meeting with his family doctor. The doctor examined Toby very slowly and carefully. He informed Toby that the markings on his back were, indeed, burn marks. Moreover, these markings were arranged in strange patterns across Toby's back. There were three different shapes: circles, squares and triangles. Inside each shape, there appeared to be some prints like hieroglyphics. Also the doctor told Toby that these curious markings had been pressed into his skin as if he had been branded in some manner. The doctor prescribed some antibiotics and gave Toby some tubes of ointment to apply daily to his burns. Toby was told that the burns would heal, but the scars and markings would most likely always remain visible.

For the next few weeks, Toby experienced vivid nightmares. He would wake up yelling and telling Mable that he had dreamed that beings were peering at him with their compound eyes and branding him again. Toby's screaming and thrashing about made it impossible for Mable to get any sleep at all. So, for the next few months, Toby had to sleep alone in the guest bedroom until he could sleep quietly through the night.

As a result of his experience, Toby never again went hunting with his brothers up at the family cabin. In fact he refused to travel any further north than Millinocket. He always made sure to have his cell phone and GPS with him (even on short trips). Actually, Toby rarely drove outside of Bangor at all. Even on those occasions, it had to be daylight and Mable always had to ride with him.

Eventually Toby became less anxious and was able to sleep fairly well again. His burns did indeed heal. However, the doctor was correct: the scars and indented markings never went away. As a result, Toby always felt that when he was branded, somehow some microchips had been inserted into his skin. For the rest of his life, Toby would feel that his every move was being monitored somehow. Toby always believed that it was just a matter of time before the beings would track him down, recapture him, and do more tests on him.

FINIS

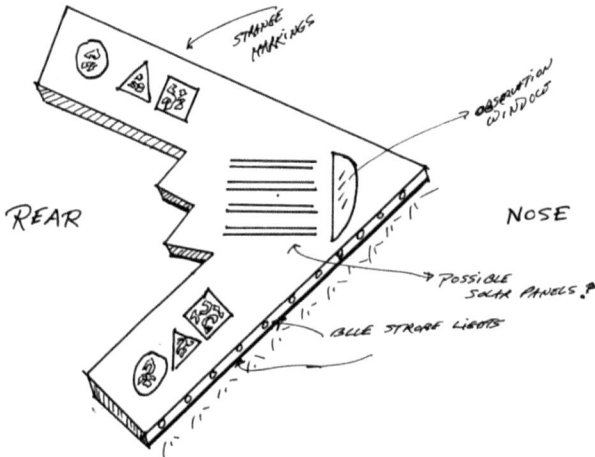

UPDATE:

As of this writing, Toby Crocker is alive and well and still living in Bangor with his wife, Mable. He is now happily retired and enjoying his two children and his three wonderful grandchildren. He adamantly refuses any requests for interviews even though he has been approached by news media ranging from The National Enquirer to 60 Minutes and Dateline. He was even contacted by Barbara Walters for one of her thirty-minute specials. To this day, Toby is very self-conscious about his back and he doesn't want anyone to stare at the strange markings on it. Therefore he wears a T-shirt at all times, even when swimming in the family pool during the hot summer months.

****

"There is a fifth dimension, beyond that which is known to man. It is a dimension between light and shadow, between science and superstition." - Rod Serling

THE CHOICE

The red Ferrari F430 Spider was speeding along the winding, cliff-side road high above the Mediterranean Sea. The driver, Max Spencer, was in great spirits. He had just won big at the Grande Casino at Monte Carlo. As a bonus, he had been in town for the famous Formula One Monaco Grand Prix. Now he was on his way to his villa in Nice where Yvette, his newest mistress, was awaiting him. "Wow! What a life. It doesn't get any better than this," he said aloud as he smiled to himself.

Suddenly, it happened. As he rounded a sharp bend in the road, he was startled to see a small boulder had fallen from the cliff above and landed on the pavement in front of him. He quickly jerked the wheel to his left. He didn't even have time to apply his brakes. However he had over-compensated and he was going way too fast. As a result, the Ferrari hit the metal guardrail and tore right through it. The car flew straight into the air, twisted violently to the right, and crashed through a thicket of trees. Finally, it came to rest upside down on the rocky ledge below. Then, for Max, everything went blank.

Miraculously, after a few minutes, he came to, breathing in thick black smoke and gasoline fumes. The front windshield had totally disintegrated and a tree limb had punctured his air bag. He was still strapped into his car. He felt streams of warm blood running down his neck and across his face. He could hardly breathe and he knew one of his lungs had been pierced. He was in agony and felt as if every one of the 206 bones in his body had been broken. Moreover, he knew with certainty that he was dying. He tried to call out for help but he couldn't move his jaw to open his mouth. He felt himself quickly losing consciousness. He felt dizzy and faint. He thought to himself, "God, I don't want to die. Please help me." He passed out within seconds.

Later, he was aware that he was actually floating in the air above the car wreckage. He felt no pain and he could actually observe all that was going on below him. He could see that his car had caught fire and that billows of black smoke were wafting upwards. Also there was the acrid odor of burning rubber. He was surprised to see that there were EMT's and other medical personnel using a Jaws of Life to cut him out of the car. They worked quickly and skillfully and eventually were able to extract him. They strapped him onto a stretcher. Then the stretcher was carefully hoisted up the sheer cliff, through the trees to the roadway above. Next, the EMT's carefully eased the stretcher into the ambulance with the flashing red and blue lights.

Now he could see that there were several police cars parked on the road high above the accident site. There was also a large fire truck and four firemen were lugging fire hoses over the side of the cliff. He could see every detail of what was happening. In addition, he could simultaneously hear all the separate conversations that were going on.

"Boy, this is the worst car wreck I've ever seen in all my years on the job," the fire chief said to one of his lieutenants. "This is even worse than the auto accident that Grace Kelly had up here back in '82."

"You got that right, Tom," the lieutenant replied. "You'd never know the car was a Ferrari except for the emblem. That baby must have been really bombin' to blow out that whole section of guardrail and land way down there. The EMT guys say it looks like this poor chap probably ain't gonna make it. Guess they can't get a pulse. This is one case where a fastened seat belt still couldn't save the driver. They were right calling this road 'Devil's Curse'."

"Do they know who this guy is?"

"Not yet. They just figure he's probably some kind of doctor. There's an MD on the license plate."

As this conversation was going on, Max Spencer began to feel himself being drawn slowly into some kind of long, dark tunnel. However, he could discern a very bright light at the far end. Despite being in this confined area, he felt no fear or anxiety. Moreover, now an interesting phenomenon was taking place. His whole life began to flash by him at a rapid pace. It seemed to him like a series of brief movie clips. Everything occurred in the correct time sequence and in minute detail. The script started with Max sitting in his high chair and ended with him entering the tunnel. He could see and hear everything he'd ever done and said....the good and the bad. What's more, during this "life review" he was given the chance to evaluate his own life. This option was far more painful for Max then being judged by another. He was sobered to see just how much his words and deeds had impacted other people during his lifetime. He never realized how mere words could be so healing or so very hurtful.

He reflected on his humble upbringing and how sad he'd felt when his mother had died when he was only seven years old, leaving his grieving father to raise him and his kid sister. He remembered how his dad had worked two jobs to get the money to send him to the state university. He wished now that he had shown his dad more love and appreciation. He thought about his teenage years and all the worry he had caused his father. He especially wished that at some point he had told his dad, "Pop, I love you." He'd give anything now to have that opportunity to go back in time and express those very words to his father, but his dad had died suddenly last winter. Now Max would never have that chance. It all came back in graphic detail. What an egocentric person he had morphed into. He wished that he had thought more about all the people who had loved him and had done so much to help him along his way.

He felt terrible about the way he had treated Carol, his first wife. They met in college and were married the summer they graduated. She had worked hard and sacrificed much of her life to help him get through med school and his internship. Due in large part to her emotional and financial support, he went on to become a very wealthy and sought-after plastic surgeon. But after twenty years of marriage and three children, he had divorced Carol and married his secretary eighteen years his junior. Carol had been left with the house and three children to raise basically by herself. He had always provided very well for them financially. However, he was rarely there emotionally or even physically for them. He had always seen them at the holidays. But that certainly didn't make up for all the times he was never there when his children had really needed a father. He had tried to make up for his absences with clothes, racing bikes, and even cars. However, nothing could make up for not being a real part of their lives. Partially as a result of his neglect over the years, all of his children had suffered with their own issues.

His oldest son, Scott, had become addicted to heroin and was in his third rehab facility. Last year he had almost died as a result of an overdose. The EMT's had managed to save him by mere seconds. Scott had told his counselors that he felt like a "total loser" who had been abandoned by his father and was taking drugs to numb the pain.

Sarah, his second child, had been born mentally challenged. She was living in a very decent group home with three other girls. Max rarely went to visit her. Therefore he now had no relationship with her.

His third child, Marc, was a freshman at Dartmouth College and was doing well. He was an exceptional athlete and a serious student who somehow seemed to be fairly well adjusted. However, he held a lot of anger toward Max for deserting the family. Max had tried several times to rekindle some kind of relationship. But Marc made it clear that he was not interested now. Too much time had passed.

Max had known for a long time that he was no Father of the Year. But now he saw that he wasn't any kind of father. Was his legacy going to consist of four homes, five cars, $30 million in cash, and a string of broken relationships with his family and friends? What a pitiful epitaph!

After this "life review" was over, he flew through the tunnel at a tremendous speed. He emerged at the other end and was immediately enveloped in a brilliant, warm light. The light was much more intense than anything he'd ever experienced on earth. He felt a sense of total fulfillment, peace and love. He knew immediately that for the first time in his life he was loved unconditionally---just the way he was! He wasn't loved for what he'd accomplished or the money that he'd made. In fact, he was still loved, despite all his selfishness and failings. This realization was too much for Max and he began to cry. He didn't cry because he was sad, but because now for the very first time, he could shed all his man-made defenses and stand naked and alone in the presence of True Love.

He felt that he was in the presence of a "Life Force" or a "Being." He knew that this "Being" knew all about him and could see into his heart. Words were not necessary for Max to communicate with this Being because they could communicate telepathically. Max also knew that the Being knew in advance what Max was going to communicate. This ability did not frighten Max. He just accepted that it was so. He knew that the Being was omniscient and knew Max better than Max knew himself.

The Being communicated a simple statement to Max: "You have had a chance to review your life. You may remain here with me. Or you may return to your life and family. Your time is on earth is not up. So you do have a choice. What do you wish to do?"

This proposal did not startle Max. He had already made up his mind.

FINIS

21

THE MOTH AND THE FLAME

The unplanned product of a one-night stand,
In the game of life, she'd been dealt a bad hand.
A lonely child with her father unknown,
The seeds of insecurity long had been sown.

She was every man's lust – every woman's dream,
But no one's life is ever as it seems.
She glittered among us for thirty-six short years
Through frenzied celebrity, champagne, pills and tears.

She knew full well just how fickle was fame,
But like the doomed moth, she was drawn to its flame.
But fame may be empty, simply gold-plated,
And it has its own danger and may be ill-fated.

She shot like a rocket to international fame,
The moth was now known by just her first name.
A few breathy words in a sequined dress,
No need to expand – we all know the rest.

But what the hell happened? What went so wrong?
First she was siren – now she's just song.
Was she just an object for every man's lust,
This platinum blonde with the world-famous bust?

Used and abused right to the end,
Sad and alone, without one true friend.
In her final days, she had nothing left to sell.
But still – there was fear of the secrets she could tell.

What really happened on that hot August night?
Did three dark figures flee from the light?
Were their footsteps on the Mexican tiles?
Had these muffled voices crossed many miles?

22

It's all smoke and mirrors, haze, fog and mist.
Her fate had now taken a perilous twist.
The room sanitized – well before dawn,
All evidence removed – Red diary now gone.

The lonely moth had flown too close to the flame - then

POOF!

In a second, she was GONE!

THE PERFECT DIVE

He sat by himself in a dimly lit booth in the empty barroom. His only company was Tony the bartender and the three empty Sam Adams bottles on the table in front of him. He had just driven back from the Cape to avoid the much-hyped impending hurricane. The ride back was quick and uneventful and there were few cars on the road. But who in their right mind would be out driving on this rainy, windy night anyway?

How fitting that there was a storm howling outside, he thought. There was also a storm raging inside his head.

Just three hours ago, his girlfriend, Patty, had broken up with him. She had told him as gently as she could that she felt that their relationship had run its course. She told him that she would always have a love in her heart for him. However, she also knew that even at his age of thirty-two he was still in no way prepared to make a serious, long-term commitment to her. She was thirty now and she wanted to marry, settle down and start a family, just as her girlfriends were doing. In fact, her last friend had just gotten married this summer. Patty knew her boyfriend was a wonderful, kind man and that he loved her. But she also knew that he was not ready to enter into a marriage. She just wasn't going to wait any longer. Four years with no ring was plenty long enough. She had wished him every happiness and told him that with his athletic good looks, great personality and high-paying, secure job as a computer analyst, he would quickly find someone else.

What she hadn't gone into was the other major complication in their relationship: his obsession with sports. He was crazy about baseball, football and ice hockey. However the real love of his life was swimming and diving. Ever since he had been taught by his dad to swim at three years old, he had become addicted to it. He had been the captain of his prep school and college swim teams. He had been to several of the Olympic Games. He even had a chance to meet Greg Louganis and have his photo taken with him. He now had a personally signed photo of the two of them on his living room wall. In fact, all the walls of his condo were covered with framed, autographed photos and all kinds of sports memorabilia. Even his bedroom and bathroom walls were plastered with sports photos. He subscribed to four sporting publications and piles of these magazines were neatly stacked on his coffee table. Even more piles of magazines were carefully arranged in rows along many of the walls. Whenever Patty came over to the condo, she told him that she experienced "sensory overload."

He smiled sadly to himself as he carefully lined up the empty beer bottles in front of him. Next, he methodically started peeling off the labels and placing them in neat little piles in front of each bottle. "Damn this OCD," he fumed. It always got worse when he got stressed out.

Six years ago he had gone to the OCD clinic at Mass General. He had been extensively tested by one of the leading experts in the country, Dr. Michael Jeneke. The official diagnosis was, indeed, Obsessive Compulsive Disorder (OCD). The prescribed medications did help somewhat. However, he was never totally symptom-free. Moreover, the fact that he had consumed three beers in a such a short period of time was not good. He was afraid that the alcohol was starting to interfere with his meds. He already felt a little light-headed and his thoughts began to feel jumbled. He hated these feelings because it made it much harder for him to make decisions.

"Hey, Tony, how about another cold one and some more popcorn?"

"Okay, pal, but that's it. You've had enough for tonight."

"Okay, sure. Don't worry," the young man replied. "I'm moving along as soon as I finish this beer."

A few minutes later, Tony returned with the beer and popcorn. Just as soon as he walked back to the bar, the lights flickered once again. The young man figured he had better get home before this storm got any worse. He finished off his small bowl of popcorn and quickly chugged his beer.

"See ya, Tony. Thanks!"

He got up slowly and headed for the door and his brand new black Toyota Rav4. It was raining so hard now he could barely discern his vehicle in the empty parking lot. He dashed to the SUV and jumped in quickly. Soaked to the skin, he slid behind the wheel, flipped on the ignition and pulled out of the lot, turning right and headed for home. He was looking forward to having a hot shower and popping in the tape of that Red Sox game he had just missed. But, then, he suddenly changed his mind. He decided that he'd go to the ultra-modern gym that he'd joined last month to practice some of his favorite dives. He really loved the two tier diving platforms that they had installed. Whenever he got really stressed out, he would revert to his swimming and diving to relax. It had never failed. Maybe after some diving and swimming, he could calm down and think of some way to win Patty back. Perhaps there was still some chance after all.

After a ten-minute ride through blinding rain, he finally turned into the driveway to the new gym. He could barely make out the form of the huge brick building that loomed up before him. Instead of parking in the lot out back, he decided to park right next to the front door. He drove over the grass and parked on the front brick walkway at an angle. He ran to the front door and pulled on the brass handle. The door was locked. Apparently they had closed early because of the storm. He decided since he was already here, he might as well go in. He swiped his card across the scanner and one of the big glass doors quickly popped open. The rain was so torrential he couldn't even make out the notices about pool times and upcoming swim meets that were taped to the glass inside the door.

The lights flickered once as he made his way to the locker room at the end of the hall. He went directly to his own locker and rummaged through his gym bag for the official Olympic Speedo that a friend of one of his swim coaches had obtained for him. It was one of his prized possessions and he always wore it. He stripped out of his sopping wet clothes and toweled off. Then he slipped on the Speedo and headed out of the locker room. All of a sudden, the lights flickered twice and went out. "Oh, great, the perfect ending of a lousy day," he muttered as he stood there in total darkness. But it appeared that the generator must have finally kicked in. Very slowly the gym was bathed in an eerie greenish-yellow light. However, it was still quite dark and he could barely discern the exercise equipment. Yet he made his way down the corridor to the pool room. He pushed open the door and walked in.

It was even darker in this big room. It seemed to him that this generator was not working very well. He stopped for a moment as a cold shudder seemed to pulse through him. Was this his imagination playing tricks on him? This would be the perfect setting for one of those low-budget horror flicks. "I can see it now," he announced to the invisible audience, "JASON MEETS THE SWIMMER AT THE POOL." He laughed out loud at his own lame joke.

26

His head started to buzz a little as he made his way to the ladder and the diving platforms. He tried to focus on his upcoming dive and crowd out any intrusive thoughts. He really hated it when alien thoughts made it hard for him to concentrate. He had to block out everything else now and prepare himself for his dives.

When he was totally focused, he was able to block out his surroundings and any noises or external distractions. He slowly climbed the ladder to the second diving platform. He focused his mind on the mechanics of this dive. It was his best dive and also his very favorite. He walked out onto the springboard and forced himself to concentrate only on this dive and nothing else. He turned around with his back to the pool. This was the back dive in the straight position. It was a Voluntary Dive with a 1.6 Degree of Difficulty (DD). He arranged his toes carefully on the diving board. He bounced up and down a few times to loosen his muscles up a little. Then he jumped on the board and sprang up in the air. He arched his back perfectly and started to descend. He closed his eyes for a second and felt the adrenalin race through him. He could sense that it was a perfect dive. And, it was! At the very last second, he opened his eyes and gasped in horror. The pool was empty! It had been completely drained. The last thing that he experienced was a brilliant flash of light. Then, everything went blank.

****

The next morning at exactly eight am, the white van from the Olympic Pool Company pulled up at the gym. The two repairmen stepped out, each carrying a cardboard carton. They were surprised to see a black Toyota Rav4 parked on the walkway by the front door. The van was plastered with wet leaves and small twigs. It appeared to have been there a long time.

"What the heck?" the older man said as he and his assistant walked to the front doors and found one of them ajar.

"Why would anyone go in here when it says right on this notice- Closed for Repairs?"

"Yeah. And who the hell would go to any gym in the middle of a hurricane? Hey, I hope that this isn't a robbery or something."

The two men cautiously entered the gym with their cartons. Everything seemed to be in order. After a quick search, they made their way down the hallway to the elaborate, new pool room.

"Okay, let's get these new drains and pool lights installed so we can make it to that Braintree job before 10:30," the older man said.

They carried their two boxes over to the edge of the pool and put them down on the tile coping. Just as they were about to descend one of the ladders, they were jolted to see the bloody, crumpled body splayed out in the deep end of the pool. Without advancing any further, it was plain to see that the handsome, young diver in the Olympic Speedo was dead.

HALFWAY AROUND THE WORLD
AND BACK IN THIRTY DAYS

The following entries were taken from a daily journal I kept during a 30-day house swap to Southeast Asia during July of 2011. I have tried to select the writings that are the most informative and perhaps entertaining. My aim is to give you a brief overview of this extended swap. Well, here we go...

On June 30th, 2011, I departed for Southeast Asia for a month long vacation with my sister, Kate, and her friend, Roger. Roger had swapped his house on a pond in Falmouth for a large apartment on the twentieth floor of a Singapore high-rise building. Roger, Kate and I were very familiar with this "house swap" process as we had done this before. We planned on using Singapore as our base and then branching out from there to visit four other countries: Thailand, Laos, Cambodia and the island of Bali in Indonesia. This extended trip had been very carefully planned out. Roger had arranged with a Singapore tour company to set up our flights, hotels, a personal driver and tour guide to meet us with our own van at the airport in each country we were going to visit. This was indeed, for me, the trip of a lifetime. I was also very fortunate to be going with two seasoned world travelers. Roger had already traveled to sixty-four countries and Kate had been to at least forty-five.

This journal is my attempt to write a daily account of our travel experiences. So, if you're ready, sit back in a comfortable chair, relax, and let me take you along on my Southeast Asian adventure!

DAY ONE:

We leave Logan Airport in Boston at 8 pm. After a six-and-one-half hour flight, we arrive at Heathrow Airport in London, England where we have a five-hour layover. Next we board another plane for our three-hour flight to Helsinki, Finland.

We arrive in Helsinki pretty much on schedule. However, we now have a six-hour layover. We find what is called the Executive Lounge.

Apparently, most airports have these lounges. For a reasonable fee, one can check in for a meal, drinks, a nice rest and even a shower. We decide we will check out this lounge and relax as we still have a long flight ahead of us. At midnight, we leave the lounge and board our FinAir flight to Singapore. This is our third flight and it will be a long one, taking eleven-and-one-half hours! This will be the longest flight that I have ever taken and I'm not really looking forward to it. By the time we get to Singapore we will have been in the air for a total of 21½ hours.

SATURDAY, JULY 2, 2011: ARRIVAL IN SINGAPORE

We arrive at Singapore Airport after a long but smooth flight. We have crossed time zones, so we are now on Singapore time. It is 5:30 pm. We are tired and really have no idea what day it is as we have lost a full day traveling.

As we walk into the Singapore Airport, I am impressed by how immaculate it is. This airport is huge, ultra-modern and clean as a whistle. Instead of tile, we are walking on wall-to-wall carpet that appears to be brand new. Not a stain or a blemish is to be seen.

The airport seems to go on forever. I later learn that the Singapore Airport is one of the nicest in the world. There is even a butterfly house and an indoor pool located in the airport.

I remember that someone told me that Singapore is a very clean city with no litter. If one drops paper or (God forbid!) gum on the street, they are levied a big fine.

Before we land, I fill out the customary disembarkment form. However, this particular form is different from other ones I've seen. In big, red block letters it says, WARNING: DEATH FOR DRUG TRAFFICERS UNDER SINGAPORE LAW! I guess that would solve the American-Mexican drug problem fast!

Kate and Roger pass smoothly through customs. However, there is a problem when I present my passport. It doesn't scan correctly. The customs lady tries it four times. Still won't scan. She's really not happy with this. Instead of typing my numbers in, she leads me over to a customs officer at a window. He looks at my passport and tells me it looks like I had put it in a washing machine, as it is wrinkled up and somewhat distorted. I explain that it got sweaty under my T-shirt in the pouch I carry it in. He types in my numbers, processes me and hands the passport back. He adds, "You're going to have trouble with this passport."

Great! I think. I have four more countries to visit and numerous airports to pass through using this same passport.

After we exit the airport, we go outside to hail a taxi. We secure a nice blue cab that is only six months old and ultra clean. The cab looks like it has never been used. The cabbie is very friendly and talkative. He says the cab companies wash their cabs every day. Also, every five years, they buy a brand new one. As we drive into the city of Singapore, I am amazed at how modern and beautiful it is.

On both sides of the highway, we see beautifully maintained bushes and multi-colored flowers in full bloom. When do they ever have time to have gardeners keep all this up? The highways are in excellent condition and look like they were just paved.

As I look out my window, I see many tall skyscrapers and modern, contemporary buildings. The architecture is almost surreal it is so exquisite. Singapore prides itself on being a modern, upscale city/state. Any old buildings are passé. Thus, Singapore is in a constant state of flux and construction. "Old is out! New is in!" Many cranes and derricks are visible on the distant horizon. Older buildings are constantly being razed and replaced with ultra-modern structures. Anyone who left Singapore twenty years ago and just returned would have trouble recognizing the place.

Soon we ride by a huge ferris wheel that is supposed to be the highest observation wheel in the world. We also pass Marina Bay Park, where Singapore's newest architectural structure has been built. We see the

31

stunning Sky Deck which looks like a huge boat or wingless plane perched atop three concave skyscrapers. This unique structure is considered one of the modern manmade wonders of the world. I've seen photos of this building in brochures and I definitely plan to check it out.

After a twenty minute ride, we arrive at the 27-story high rise that is to be our home base for the next thirty days. We enter the gated complex and are driven to the front door of our building. We thank our driver, pay our fare and lug our suitcases into the foyer. We then take the elevator to the twentieth floor, go down the hallway and knock at a huge, carved, wooden door. The door is opened by Eliyia, a young Indonesian, Muslim girl in her thirties. She is the resident nanny/housekeeper for the family living here.

Eliyia (or Elvira as Kate and I call her between ourselves) ushers us through a foyer and then into a huge living room with a wall of large glass windows overlooking a part of Singapore and the Singapore River. What a view! This apartment is massive, consisting of seven or eight rooms, four bedrooms, three-and-a-half baths. It is very cheerful and beautifully decorated with many artifacts from Southeast Asia and other countries. My bedroom has its own private bath. The room is large with two bunk beds and a single twin bed. This is the girls' room as the owners have three girls and two boys (ages from eight to thirteen). I quickly select the bottom bunk that is about six inches in front of a huge window overlooking the Singapore skyline. I figure this view will be even more spectacular at night when the whole city lights up.

After we all unpack and rest a bit, we decide to go out to get some supper. Roger takes us to a food court where he has eaten before. It is a ten-minute walk from our room. The food court is quite large and clean with food offerings from many Asian countries. There are all kinds of rice, beef, chicken, fresh vegetables, fish, soups and other fine choices. One can order Singapore, Korean, Indian, Vietnamese and many other types of meals...all at a very reasonable prices. I decide on a Thai meal consisting of rice, fresh greens and some sliced chicken for only $4.50 in Singaporean money. I also decide to try a local Tiger beer for $4.00. This food court is a great place to obtain a good, nutritious meal for a low price. The regular Singaporean restaurants are fairly expensive. The local supermarket foods are also very expensive. Ninety percent of

Singaporean food is imported. Therefore, the cost of importing is passed onto the local consumer. I notice that a small bottle of Conchay Toro Chilean wine is $31.00 Singaporean money. At home, this same bottle would be about $8.00.

We enjoy our first meal in Singapore and take a leisurely walk back to our apartment. We unpack the rest of our luggage. I take a shower in the private bathroom, put on my pajamas and crawl into my cozy "bunk with a view." I quickly drift off to sleep looking out at a panoramic view of Singapore at night with all the lights. So ends my first day in this interesting city.

SUNDAY, JULY 3, 2011: STROLLING THROUGH CHINATOWN

I wake up in my comfortable twin bunk bed. I see through my window that it is a bright, sunny day. I wander out to the living room and have breakfast with Kate and Roger. I look around the huge living and dining room and notice all the interesting pieces of furniture and the many wall decorations.

In the dining room, there is a gigantic porcelain vase that is as tall as I am. I wonder how they ever got the thing into this apartment. There are several large, round brass gongs w/mallets on the walls. There is even a picture that was drawn by an elephant! Apparently, they do have elephants that can draw fairly good pictures if they are carefully trained. In fact, there are two 4"x6" photos included in the frame showing the elephant doing this particular drawing. Amazing!

As I wander around the rooms, I see many pictures of the family that lives here. It is evident from all these family photos that this is a very close family that does as much with their children as they can. There is even a photo of all five kids on a camel in Dubai. I think it is so great that these kids are exposed to so much. Roger tells me that the father has a very good job as a computer software manager. This is his second house swap to Roger's home on the Cape. What a great summer for these children, enjoying a house on a nice, clean, swimmable pond on the Cape.

After breakfast, we decide to take a walk to Chinatown to do some sightseeing and shopping. Chinatown is huge and crowded with many stores and roadside booths. You can buy almost anything here. The prices are very reasonable and items here cost far less than at the regular stores. I see many solar-powered, waving cats. Apparently,

33

these are very popular with the tourists. Naturally, I have one on my desk back home now. Watches are another big item. There are real Rolex watches for up to $600.00 or more. However, there are very good fake ones for as little as $25.00. Scarves are one of the biggest sellers. There are thousands of scarves in beautiful colors and designs. These are made of real silk, not polyester. It is hard to walk very far without being approached to buy one. The prices are incredibly reasonable. Needless to say, we all returned home with many beautiful, pure silk scarves to give as gifts.

After a few hours, it is time for lunch. We stop and eat at an authentic Chinese restaurant called Fatty Weng's. I had a wonderful roasted chicken lunch. The waiter was very comical so I had my picture taken with him. When I finally developed it, I saw that he was holding up two fingers behind my head. All the people we meet on this trip are very helpful and friendly. The one rude person I did encounter was another tourist.

Before we leave Chinatown, we wander into some tailor shops. There are many of these shops where you can have a custom, tailored silk suit made for a very low price. The prices start out at about $250 or so. However, you can get a beautiful man's suit for $120.00 or less. These suits are made of real silk, not a synthetic fabric. Also you get a chance to pick from a range of truly beautiful colors. I almost bought one. However, now that I'm retired, I rarely wear a suit anymore.

Our next stop is a Hindu temple. Outside, the temple is decorated with very elaborate carved, painted figures. The detail and colors are really amazing. After viewing the outside, we are allowed to enter.

However, we must first remove our shoes and women must be properly covered. Therefore, Kate was advised to wear a longish skirt and a blouse that covered her upper arms. We find that this "dress code" is pretty standard in

34

most of Buddhist or Hindu temples that we visit during this trip. We are not allowed to take photos inside this particular temple. However, it is well worth the time to go inside and see the ornate, gold-leaf carvings. After viewing the interior of the temple, we walk back to our apartment. This China town trip took about six hours and we walked about four miles. So ends are first full day in Singapore.

MONDAY, JULY 4, 2011: LUCKY'S DEPARTMENT STORE AND RAFFLE'S HOTEL

Wow! It is the Fourth of July! I look out my window and see that it is another bright, sunny day here in Singapore. We decide that we need to go to the travel agency to get the necessary paperwork for our upcoming twelve-day tour to Thailand, Laos and Cambodia. So, after breakfast, we walk to the travel agency that Roger used to book this next part of our trip (Country Travel). We meet with Tih who gives us our brochures, schedules, and other printed papers we will need for the next part of our traveling. After leaving the travel bureau, Roger suggests that we check out Lucky's Mart.

We take a short cab ride to this unique shopping center. I am amazed when we exit the cab and enter this grand department store. This store has seven stories. There are escalators going to each level. This place sells everything it seems. Many signs say 'Three for $10.00.' When you barter, you can sometimes get four or five for $10.00. There are racks and stacks of T-shirts. We quickly learn that Singapore sizing is different from US sizing. Our idea of an extra-large, would be XXX large or Super-Size to a Singaporeans.

Whenever, I went to buy a T-shirt, they would quickly say, "Supersize this way!" This worked out okay, however, it did make me feel like a Sumo wrestler every time I wandered into a clothing store. As a result, I DID try to eat a little less. Between the rice and low-fat meals, the miles of walking, and the perspiring from the humid climate, I lost twelve pounds. After we leave Lucky's, we stop at an Asian restaurant and have an Indian meal of curry chicken, rice, beans and greens. Good and low fat.

After a light supper, we decide that we will take a cab to Raffle's Hotel. We call for a cab from our apartment. In two minutes, it is waiting for us in front of our building. Apparently, the cabbie was right around the corner. At any rate, we are dropped off in front of Raffle's

Hotel. It is a huge building that appears to take up a few blocks. It is a very elegant, white stone structure. We meet the doorman who is dressed in an ornate white suit and what looks like a Punjab headpiece. He is supposed to be the most photographed man in Singapore. Yes, I have my picture taken with him!

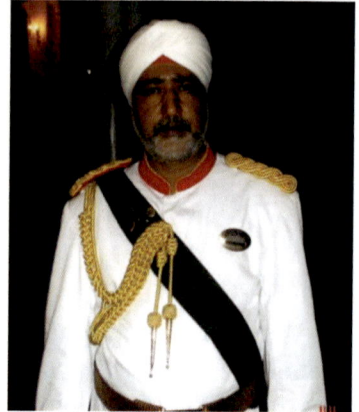

After we go inside, we walk around and stare in wonder. Everything looks like it is white marble. There are ornate chandeliers and curving stairways. There are many high-end shops, boutiques, etc. The room rates are very high, if you can even get one. I'm told the rates range from $500 to $5000 per night. Michael Jackson and Elizabeth Taylor reserved a whole floor when Michael was here for a concert about ten years ago. I buy a copy of a large, brass room key tag for $15.00.

We all go to the Long Bar where the first official "Singapore Sling" was concocted. Naturally I decide to have one since this is the famous bar where the first drink was made. The drink was $25.00 and it was not worth the price. The drink came in a small, Bloody Mary type glass. It was, indeed, a very disappointing drink with a pinkish color and tasted like some kind of fruit drink. It was way too sweet and if there was any booze in it, I couldn't taste it. Oh, well, live and learn. We ate a lot of peanuts that were in small bowls on the table. Apparently, the tradition is to eat the peanuts and throw the shells on the floor. You are not supposed to leave them on the table, I guess. Anyway, we did eat the nuts and did our best to throw the broken shells on the floor. When in Singapore, do as the Singaporeans do! All told, we were at the Raffles Hotel from 6 pm 'til 8:45 pm.

TUESDAY, JULY 5, 2011: ARRIVAL IN BANGKOK AND ATTACK OF THE KIDNEY STONES

We leave Singapore aboard Singapore Airlines. This airline is absolutely beautiful! The plane is huge and in pristine condition. The seats are very roomy and comfortable. The flight attendants are beautiful young girls who look like China dolls. Beautiful faces. Every hair in place. Dressed in gorgeous kimono-type dresses. I find out later

36

that Singapore Airlines is the best airline in the world, and I can see why. We arrive in Bangkok Airport about two hours later.

After we leave the airport, we meet our personal guide named Tick. We take our luggage and follow him outside to the big, white van with our driver. The van is air-conditioned and quite comfortable. We are each given a cold bottle of water and a nice, cold, clean facecloth to wipe our faces. It is very sunny and very hot. The temperature is about 90 and the humidity around ninety percent! We are driven to our hotel in Bangkok. There is a lot of traffic and it is slow-moving and congested.

Our hotel is a very authentic, old style palace. The door attendant and receptionist bow to us with their hands in a prayer position as we check in. We soon see that this is a common way of greeting a person in Thailand. We learn how to fold our hands (like in praying), bow our heads and say Hello (Sa-wadi-dee-kobb, phonetically). Thank you is Kobb Khun (phonetically).

We are shown to our room, which is quite decent. There is one Queen-size bed and one twin bed (mine). We are happy to see that the room is air-conditioned. We then had a nice lunch at the hotel. After lunch, we get into the van with Tick to go see the Grand Palace and its grounds.

On the way there, Roger has a serious kidney stone attack. He is riding in the seat behind Kate and me. He says he is in terrible pain and he has to lie down on his seat. His face is very red and he is perspiring a lot. At first I think that he is having a heart attack. He insists that it is a kidney stone attack and that this has happened before.

He has severe pain in his back, one of the symptoms of kidney stones. We ask Tick to take us to the hospital immediately. I ask him how far the hospital is. He tells me that it is about twenty minutes.

We are stuck in terrible traffic and are making extremely slow progress. About fifteen minutes later, I ask him how far away we are now. He says, "Twenty minutes." I remind him that he told me that fifteen minutes ago. At this rate, we will be lucky to get to the hospital in another hour! This traffic snarl is incredible. If someone were actually having a heart attack, they would be long dead before they got to the hospital. Meanwhile, Roger says that he is feeling better and needs to get some fresh air.

We finally find a place to pull over and Roger gets out and walks

37

around a bit. Soon he feels much better and says he doesn't need to go to the hospital. He gets back into the van and we proceed to see the Grand Palace and grounds.

The palace is truly amazing and covered with gold-leaf inside and out. I have never seen so much gold leaf and beautiful mosaic work. With the combination of gold and the bright, red, blue and green mosaic tiles, it is truly awe-inspiring.

We saw the Reclining Buddha which is all gold, huge and eighty-one feet long. It is so large that they had to build a temple around it. We see many glittering spires and statues and a large model of Angkor Wat, which we will visit in Cambodia. We saw the temple where the famous Emerald Buddha is showcased. However, they were doing repair work so we couldn't get in.

After viewing the palace, temples, Buddhas and the grounds, we saw a short film about the royal barges. The film was excellent and it showed footage of the elaborate gold barges in the water during important official events involving the king and other Thai royalty.

We went into the museum where artisans were very carefully doing gold leaf work and painting on the actual, original barges. The close up detail was truly amazing! We took a canal tour around the grounds of the Grand Palace. Next we went out onto the Chao Phraya River and visited Wat Arun, the magical 'Temple of Dawn,' with its beautiful pagoda decorated with multi-colored porcelain fragments.

WEDNESDAY, JULY 6, 2011: JIM THOMPSON'S HOUSE AND THE SOLID GOLD BUDDHA

We all get up around 6:30. Tick is going to be picking us up at eight to take us to visit the Jim Thompson house. We arrive at breakfast at 7:08 am. No one else has even arrived yet. We get our coffee and juice and sit down for a minute to wake up. There is a wonderful selection of hot and cold food and we have an excellent breakfast.

After we are done, we go into the lobby where Tick is waiting. We get into the van and go to Jim Thompson's house. Apparently, Jim Thompson disappeared very mysteriously and the case still has not been solved. The house is a very authentic, Thai-style home that was built around 1800. Many of the furnishings and artifacts are original. Jim Thompson was a world-traveler and collector of fine art. We are given a nice tour of this home. Jim Thompson is famous in Thailand because he was responsible for developing and improving methods of making original Thai silk. After the tour, we are encouraged to explore the grounds on our own. There are stone walkways, beautiful gardens and pools full of Koi fish and Lotus flowers. We end up staying over an hour at the Thompson estate.

Next, we are driven to see another Buddhist temple. This temple is important because it houses the solid gold Buddha. This Buddha is truly amazing and I can see why it is so famous. It is huge, 100% gold, and weighs about 5½ tons! Apparently, years ago, some laborers were moving what they thought was a stone Buddha statue. They accidentally dropped it and a huge crack opened up. They immediately saw that the stonework on the exterior covered a solid gold statue within. This was a hugely important discovery at the time.

We saw even more Buddhas on this tour. After all this, we were "Buddha'd out" and were glad to move on to something else. We took a

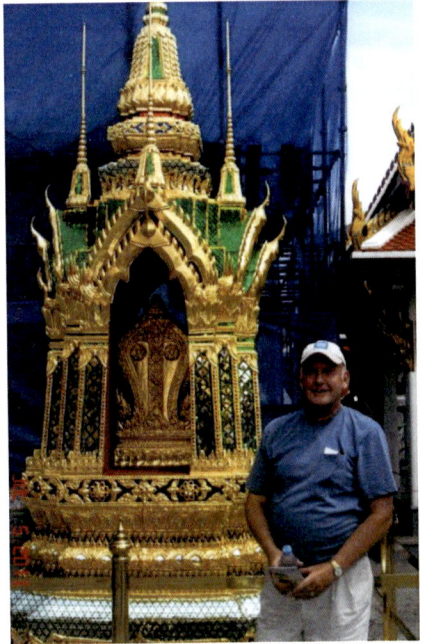

cab back to our hotel. Our guide came along to show our cabbie where are hotel was. He got out with us and walked us across the street. The traffic in Bangkok is very heavy and they drive really fast. Crossing a street can be hazardous to one's health.

At this point, we are all tired. It is very hot and humid and we are glad to be in the central air conditioning in our hotel room. We have been going at a pretty fast pace. We decide to relax and take a nap, then we have supper at a real authentic Thai restaurant. We are directed to The Mango Tree. We all have a delicious meal with wonderful fresh vegetables. After dinner, Kate decides to go for a massage. Her plan is to get one in each country that we visit. Roger and I go back to our hotel.

Tomorrow will be another busy day. Tick will be picking us up at 5:30 am to take us to the airport. We are flying to Chaing-Kai in Northern Thailand.

FRIDAY, JULY 8, 2011: PHIL MEETS A PYTHON AND A BOA

We leave Bangkok about 8:30 am. Two hours later, we arrive in Chaing-Kai (Northern Thailand). We are met by our new guide and driver in another white van. It is extremely hot and humid as usual. We are given bottles of cold water and more cold, wet facecloths to cool us off. It works!

Soon after our arrival, we board a typical longtail boat for the one-hour ride to some small but interesting villages along the Kok River. We stop at Baan Ruammit, a fair-sized Karen village. The Karen is the hill tribe group in Thailand. Many photos of this tribe have appeared in the pages of National Geographic magazine. This is the tribe that features the "long-necked women" who have the big brass rings around their necks. It appears that their necks are very long. The truth is that they appear

that way because their shoulder bones are pushed down due to constantly wearing these heavy brass rings. When a girl is about thirteen years old, she receives her first ring. A ring is added every few years until she is around thirty-five and has a total of twelve or more rings. The women wear very bright, colorful silk clothes. The young girls are artfully made up and very attractive. These people are very poor and live in very humble, rustic conditions. They offer many beautiful, homemade scarves and other items for sale at very low prices. We end up buying some things that we really don't want or need. However, we feel that we should try to give them something. One cannot just hand them money because that encourages begging.

After we leave the Karens, we continue down the Kok River to see an elephant preserve.

Even though it is extremely hot, we can keep fairly cool with our bottled water. Kate and I elect to ride an elephant. We got up on the platform and sat on the small, chair-like structure on the elephant's back. There is a man up there with us who guides the elephant. We ride for about fifteen minutes while the elephant wades out into the muddy river to get a drink. We see many piles of elephant dung and learn that this dung is used to make a very important type of wrinkly paper.

41

As we are leaving the elephant camp, we come across a section where there are different kinds of snakes. A man asks me if I would like my photo taken with a python and boa constrictor wrapped around me. Without thinking, I say, "Sure."

The man tells me to hold out both my hands with my palms up. A Boa Constrictor is placed around my neck and the ends are placed in my hands. This snake is very heavy and its scales feel like cool plastic. To top it off, a Python is casually draped around my neck. Sooo nice! A photo is snapped and within five minutes the two snakes are removed from me. GOOD!

We stop and look around the snake section. I pick up the 8"x10" photo about fifteen minutes later. How the heck did they develop this picture so fast way out in the middle of nowhere?

Next, we get back into our longtail boat and go back onto the Kok River. We return the way we came so the ride is about one hour or so. It is extremely hot (90 degrees) and very humid. We drink more of our bottled water and use the cold face cloths. Then we arrived at the section called 'The Golden Triangle'. This is where the three countries of Thailand, Laos and Myanmar (Burma) meet. It is a famous focal point and I have my photo taken in front of a sign saying "Golden Triangle." I also have my picture taken in front of the archway leading into the country of Myanmar although we do not enter.

We now return to our hotel. This has been a very high energy, fast-paced trip. What a full day! However, we have learned a lot. We go to bed exhausted but happy! Tomorrow will be a whole new adventure.

SATURDAY, JULY 9, 2011: THE WORST HOTEL IN THE WORLD

We leave our lodge (cabin) on the Mekong at 8 am. Then we board a barge for Laung Probang. After about an hour, the barge moors and we disembark and meet our new guide. His name is Julian and he is a friendly, happy soul. It seems that he is always smiling and laughing. We get into the customary white, air-conditioned van and have a cold drink and use the cold face cloths. Our young driver's name is Mr. Honda. We arrive at our new hotel. It is absolutely horrible inside and out. The foyer is small, cramped and dingy. The 'receptionist' ignores us and is busy playing Solitaire on her computer. The two men at the reservation desk don't greet us and don't seem to know what's going on. We are finally given our room key by the unfriendly receptionist. She immediately returns to her computerized card game.

We go down the hallway to find our room. The hallway is very dark and dirty. The carpeting is torn and badly stained. There are small area rugs pushed up against the outside of the doors to the rooms that we pass. We enter our room. What a disappointment! There is a queen-sized bed and one very small cot-like bed. The large bed has some kind of canopy top with a wobbly frame. The whole bed seems to sway back and forth if one touches it. The coverlet (or spread) is torn in several places. What's worse, there are no actual drapes on the windows! There is some kind of sheer, filmy thing covering it. So, essentially anyone outside can pretty much see into this elegant boudoir. As Betty Davis would say, "What a dump!"

Roger goes downstairs to the foyer. He explains patiently that we cannot stay here. He goes on to explain that he has traveled to sixty-four countries and that this is the worst hotel that he has ever been in! He explains that we were told that this was going to be a four-star hotel. The hotel manager proudly tells us that they have just received their first star! Roger says that this place is totally unacceptable. He phones Julian and quickly explains the problem. In about half an hour, Julian returns to pick us up from the hotel in an even bigger, nicer van. We get in the new van and within a few minutes we arrive at our new hotel that is actually only a few buildings away on the same street.

This hotel REALLY is a 4-star hotel! It is absolutely gorgeous. Beautiful foyer. Huge room. Large bathroom with a big, tiled shower and glass doors. We are all very happy and relieved. We walk down the street to the famous Night Market in Laung Probang. Very nice and up-scale set up. Wares are neatly displayed. Many gorgeous, authentic silk scarves. Beautiful bags of different kinds. Very nice pieces of jewelry. Prices are very low and the quality is very high. I wish that I had a larger family to buy gifts for. We meander through this interesting market. We buy some items and then go back to our nice hotel. We leave a message for a wake-up call at 4:45AM. Then we go to sleep quickly. There is a very heavy rain during the night. I snored loudly and woke Roger up.

SUNDAY, JULY 10TH, 2011: ANOTHER STEAMY DAY IN LAUNG PROBANG

We receive our wakeup call promptly at 4:45 am. We have breakfast. Julian picks us up and we get into the nice air-conditioned, white van again. Julian tells us about Laos. Laos is one of the poorest countries in the world. The average yearly income is about $33.00 in US money! The main crops are tea, banana, cotton, long-grain rice, lowland rice, papaya, mangos and lots of corn. There are lots of rubber and teak plantations. The history is very interesting. Time and again we are reminded how lucky we all are to have been born in the USA. The poorest person on welfare in this country lives like a king compared to these poor people.

We look at hundreds of Buddhas of all descriptions. We learn that if the Buddha has his hands/arms pointing straight down, he wants rain. If Buddha's hands are outstretched with the palms up, he's asking for peace. Again, it is a VERY hot day (95 degrees and humid). We go to lunch at a nice sidewalk café overlooking the Mekong. This lunch is provided by the tour and it is very good. We all have the fish soup w/coconut milk, fresh greens, cashew nuts with chicken and papaya salad. Of course we also have large bottles of chilled water and are supplied with cold, wet facecloths. Roger and I each had a bottle of Beer Lao, Dark, which is excellent!

We get back into the air-conditioned van and go to the Traditional Arts and Ethnology Centre that presents a history of the various ethnic groups that make up the country. We learn that there are many diverse ethnic divisions, roots and traditions that compose Laos. We see many traditional costumes and tools. We are glad to leave the center though because there is no AC.

The next stop is a visit to a large temple located at the top of a high cliff. There are 328 steps to get to the top. We quickly decide not to climb the steps to visit this Buddhist temple. We've all seen more than enough temples on this tour. We decide to take the van back to the hotel because we are really hot and tired now.

We quickly fall asleep. We all wake up roasting because the AC has broken. Kate goes out to the pool and reads. Roger goes to the desk and explains the problem. We are quickly transferred to another nice room with AC. All is good again.

Later on we go out to use the computers at the Internet Café down the street. I cannot get my e-mails so I use Facebook. As always, it is extremely hot and humid. Suddenly a big rainstorm springs up. Not unusual since this is still the rainy season. We duck into a restaurant for supper. This ends up being the worst meal we have all had on this trip. The rain has ended, so we walk to the famous Night Market again. We all buy more items then return to our cool hotel room and go to bed. So ends another full day.

MONDAY, JULY 11, 2011: ROGER'S BIRTHDAY

We get up about seven. Breakfast at eight. Julian picks us up at nine. Another adventure to come. We spend from nine to noon at a silk making textile plant. We pick out our own dyes and we each have a custom silk scarf made for us to take home. All the dyes used are natural. Great array of colors. Kate tried the silk spinning and weaving machine. The girls here work eight-hour days and only take home between $50 and $100 per week, yet, this is considered a good wage job for a woman. There are no schools to learn this. All these young girls learn this trade from their mothers.

We go to lunch across the street in a hotel restaurant. Great atmosphere, average food. After this lunch, we leave to visit two villages: The Ban Xom (traditional Lao Loum village) and Ban Na Quan, a small village of a hill-tribe group "Hmong", probably the best-known minority group in Laos.

We see that these are, indeed, very poor people. We feel like we are again walking through the pages of National Geographic. The children are truly beautiful. Kate talks with the children a little and she takes many photos.

Next we go to lovely Kuangsi Waterfalls. We have our picture taken with a Tibetan monk with the falls in the background. We see a group of happy, young people swinging on a rope and jumping into the water below the falls. Very peaceful setting. Julian presents Roger with a nice, chocolate birthday cake plus a button-down silk shirt! This is Roger's second cake as the hotel also delivered one to our room.

We eat our cake at a table next to the falls. Afterwards, we go to a bear preserve and see a large, black bear resting in his hammock swing. We visit another village where they grow cotton and weave it on looms. Later, I take Roger out for his birthday. We have a great Lao supper at the Pavilion Restaurant down the street. The two Laotian waiters sang Happy Birthday to Roger. Afterwards, we return to our hotel and go to bed early.

TUESDAY, JULY 12, 2011

Julian, our guide, will "collect" us at 11:30 am to take us to the airport to catch our flight to Vietenem (the capital of Laos).

At the airport in Vietenem, we are met by our new guide named "King Kong." He is a very little guy...Not a goliath at all. The driver of our newest white van is Mr. Wam.

The population of Laos is about 7,000,000 souls. 700,000 people live in Vietenem. 70% of population is Buddhist. 20% are Animists. We go to see the 'Temple of many Buddhas' and the Emerald Buddha. We learn that Buddha (Sidarter Guatama) died in India in 453 BC or 543 BC. We next see the Victory Gate which is half Arch De Triumphe and half Taj Mahal. This is apparently a VERY important monument. We were going to see some market place but it is closed. About 5:30 pm, we arrive at the Lao Plaza Hotel. This is a REAL five-star hotel located in a really depressing city. We have a gorgeous room with three beds all in a row. There is a pool, sauna, etc. in this hotel. Kate says that this city reminds her of Moscow...only more depressing.

WEDNESDAY, JULY 13, 2011

We enjoy our time inside the hotel. However, when we walk around the city we all find it very gloomy, grey and dingy. We feel that we are always being watched...and we probably are! All the people seem to be tired, sad and joyless looking. Mr. Wam drives us to airport and we get on a depressing, tired looking airplane with sad looking stewardesses.

We are glad to be leaving this awful place. We are so grateful that we were born here in the USA! We are certainly a very blessed country (and people)! On the plane we are served the worst plane meal that I have ever had (a cupcake and a sausage wrapped in something). I found out they call this thing a hot dog.

We stop at Pak Se for a thirty-minute layover. We get on another plane to Cambodia. So far we have flown approximately half-way around the world.

THURSDAY, JULY 14, 2011: THE MAJESTY OF ANGKOR WAT

We are all very excited to be going to Cambodia! I've always wanted to see Angkor Wat (one of the seven man-made wonders of the world). We learn that the population of Cambodia is about fourteen million people. Average yearly income is $700 to $800 a year. Population is about 90% Buddhist and 2 % Christian. We are arriving during the hot, humid Monsoon season which runs from May until October. We learn a man's lifespan is about 55-65, a woman's is 65-75. Eighty percent of the people are farmers. Rice is the main crop.

About 100,000 people worked to build Angkor Wat and it took about fifty years. "Angkor" means "village area." "Wat" means "temple." Angkor Wat was built in the years 850-1100 AD. It is the largest religious area in the world, a UNESCO HERITAGE site. Even today it is used by both Buddhists and Hindus. We see many Buddhist monks in the saffron (orange- colored) robes.

Soon we check into a beautiful four-star hotel (Tara Angkor). This is another super, modern hotel with indoor pool, spa, etc.

We get up at seven am. There was a HUGE breakfast buffet that took up the whole room! After breakfast, Mr. Mum (driver) and our guide pick us up in the lobby. We are on our way to Angkor Wat.

It is so impressive as you pull up to the complex. Kate thought the site was even more impressive than Machu Picchu. This is the biggest religious site in the world and it takes up hundreds of acres. As I mentioned, these temples are used by both Buddhists and Hindus. There are countless stone temples interconnected with many passageways. Many of the temples are covered with vines and moss. In some cases, three hundred-year-old trees have enveloped the walls and parts of the temples.

I took many pictures. Problem is you can only get a small section of the complex in each photo. There are many hieroglyphics carved into the stones. We see two Buddhist monks with the saffron robes. Roger, Kate and I had our photos taken with them. We take two great pictures (great for a screen-saver). Next, the monks asked us to take their picture with their digital cameras. Real contrast here with the ancient and modern world. It is extremely humid (97%). My clothes are totally soaked.

Eventually clouds roll in. It gets very dark and looks like rain. We continue on our tour of some of the ruins. Then, a downburst! We huddle in a temple with several other tourists until the storm passes. We start to head home to change our clothes.

Before we can get to our air-conditioned vans, scores of woman and children descend upon us to buy their wares. I buy a bag and a nice light blue, cotton T-sheet with a picture of Angkor Wat on it.

We get into our big, white KIA and head off to a really nice Cambodian restaurant. I have duck soup, chicken, pumpkin puree, green beans, bacon pieces and bananas. It was one of best lunches that we have had so far. After lunch, Mr. Mum and our guide pick us up and take us to Angkor Thom (the largest temple at this incredible site). We see the temple where The Temple of Doom was filmed starring Angelina Jolie. Angelina adopted a Cambodian boy a few years back. She has given a lot of money to the country of Cambodia and she is very well thought of here.

We continue to tour the various temples (there are scores and scores of them). It is impossible to see them all. Eventually we leave Angkor Thom because we have to go back to our hotel to change into decent clothes to see a dinner show.

About an hour later, the van picks us up and we are driven to the restaurant for a great meal and a chance to see the famous Aspara dancing girls. The young girls come out in their native costumes. All the girls are artfully made up and very beautiful. We all sit at a long table set up on the floor. We sit on cushions and place our legs into the open slots under the table. We have some good Merlot wine. We have a very good meal consisting of spring rolls, rice, sushi and other fresh vegetables. We eat while watching the show. Male and female dancers act out stories and myths. The show lasts about two hours and is well worth the time to see.

We take the van back to our hotel and go to bed about ten. We have to get some sleep because we have to be ready for our 4:30 am wake-up call. We are getting picked up at five am by our guide to go back to see the sunrise over Angkor Wat. I'm looking forward to this famous photo–op.

TUESDAY, JULY 19, 2011: CRYING AT THE EMBASSEY AND ARRIVAL IN BALI

Dear Diary: Well… The day started off great. We all got up at 5:30 and left our condo at 6:30 so that we would be at the airport by 7 am. However, our flight to Bali does not leave until 9:15 am. We take a cab and pay $34.00 US. We lug our suitcases to the counter and the check in; a woman starts to process us. The woman flips through Kate's passport four times and tells Kate that she cannot use this passport because there is no blank page for the upcoming Bali visa that we are going to be getting. Kate explains that she has two blank pages at the end of the heavily stamped passport. The check-in woman says those two pages are not any good because it doesn't have the word "Visa" at the top of the pages. The woman says this will be a BIG problem in Bali because they are very strict about this and Kate will not be able to get in. The ticket agent says we need to go back to the American Embassy in Singapore and get blank pages added to Kate's passport. Apparently the embassy is back where we just came from.

It takes half an hour by cab. By the time we get back, we will have missed our plane. The next available flight to Bali doesn't leave until

12:30. Also, this second plane will have to stop at Jakarta and cost us more money. This plane trip will take a lot longer. Meanwhile we have our private guide expecting us with his van at the Bali Airport at 12:30.

This is a real mess! Now we will have to take another cab back the way we came to get to the embassy when it opens at 8:30AM. It is now 8:05 am. The agent says that if we get added blank pages and make it back by 11:30 she can get us on the 12:30 flight to Jakarta. We will have a two-hour layover in Jakarta. Then we will take the two-hour flight to Bali, missing our guide at the airport. We have no choice if we want to see Bali. Sooooo.......We contact our guide and reschedule our meeting and add another day (and hotel night) to our itinerary because now we really have lost most of a full day. Brother!

We leave Singapore Airport at 8:05 am and take another cab back to where we started from. Half hour later we arrive back at the American Embassy just as it is opening its doors. Kate goes in and comes out crying forty minutes later. An Embassy official tells Kate she will have to pick up her passport with additional blank pages tomorrow! The price is $80.00 US for twenty blank pages! Kate explains that we have to be back at the airport by 11:00 am today! We have a plane booked and also have a guide and hotel rooms booked in Bali. Kate started to cry in the embassy.

One of the officials seemed to feel bad for her and told Kate to return in an hour at ten. Kate starts to cry again, leaves the building, and meets Roger and me outside. She explains the scenario and we all decide to get something to eat and return at 10:00 and (hopefully) obtain the passport with the new pages.

Kate goes back inside the embassy at ten o'clock and they give her back her passport with the new pages added. We take another taxi back to the airport. This taxi ride costs $10.00 more than the last ride, which covered the same route. Go figure. We arrive back in time and obtain our new tickets. We board our plane and take off about 12:30. This particular plane is awful: so cramped that you cannot move in your seat. The food is horrible and really inedible. Kate says it is the worst food she has had in all her flights to fifty countries. Thankfully, the flight is only fifty-five minutes. We disembark in Jakarta and wait an hour-and-a-half for our next flight to Bali.

We board the plane (La Guardia Airlines), which is quite nice. However, the food is as bad as what the other plane offered. I cannot even get the Jell-O out of my cup with a spoon or fork! I give up and have bottled water.

We arrive in Bali about 6:45 pm and are met by our new guide named Made. He is a Balinese man wearing a sarong and some kind of Punjab headgear. He and the driver take us in the customary white van to our hotel. On the way, we use the cold hand towels provided and drink the bottled water. As usual, it is hot. Our new hotel is called, MATAHARI TERBIT, BALI. The location is convenient and central.

The area is very dusty and touristy. There appears to be much litter around the streets. My room is okay, however, the AC does not work very well. Kate and Roger's room is much nicer with a glassed-in shower and strong AC. There is also a pool in front of their unit. There is a nice open-air restaurant but few people around and there's a small beach but it is nothing great. One has to step over an eroded embankment to get down to it. We go to the office and get our ticket vouchers for the free breakfast tomorrow morning. I go back to my room and watch TV. Surprisingly there are sixty-three channels. I'm tired so I go to bed around nine in one of the twin beds in my room.

WEDNESDAY, JULY 20TH, 2011: CHECKING OUT BALI

Aha, my first day on the island of Bali. I think of South Pacific and the song "Bali Hai." So far this doesn't look like the movie setting to me. I rise at seven and shower and shave. I met Kate and Roger at 8:30 for a really nice breakfast in the open-air restaurant. After breakfast, I got to the office to store my passport in their "wooden" safe deposit boxes.

On the way back to my room, I notice little boxes made of palm leaves. Inside each little box is a small amount of rice, pieces of banana, etc. Some boxes hang on branches. There is a box hanging next to the door of each unit (motel type units). There was one small leaf box left on the sand on the beach. I almost stepped on it! The food in these boxes is to appease the "good spirits and the bad spirits." Birds and animals end up eating the food offerings. If a rat eats it, that is not all bad because YOU may come back as a rat in the next life. They are big into reincarnation cycles it seems. Moral is, you'd better be good to all rodents, birds, etc. These Balinese folks are Hindus.

We learn that there are 4,000,000 people on the island of Bali. There are also 4,000,000 motor bikes. There are only about 400,000 cars. The motor bikes are everywhere and they are a real menace. The main roads are narrow, windy and clogged with motor bikes. I don't think they have any driver's test to drive these bikes. I think if you are seventeen, you are ready to hop on one and drive off!

We go out to lunch at a nice, open-air sports bar type restaurant. We all had American food and it was very good. Next we go out and look around to find a decent place to stay for our extra night (there are no available units in our hotel/motel). We checked out a SUPER unit in a private place that was really incredible. We would have our own, private villa with a live-in housekeeper! And the price was low.

Later that evening we went to a Balinese restaurant for dinner. It was really a great experience and evening. Kate got up and danced twice with one of the Balinese dancing girls. They wanted me to get up and dance. Roger and I decided we would rather just watch. The Balinese food was very good. After dinner Kate, Roger and I had our picture taken with two Balinese dancing girls. They told us to place our hands in the praying position. I had this photo enlarged and framed. I'm looking at it now on the wall as I type this. We go back to our hotel (motel) and I go to bed early. Tomorrow will be another busy day!

TUESDAY, JULY 26, 2011: ATTACKED BY A FLYING SQUIRREL

We go slowly today. We all get up around 9 am and enjoy a late breakfast. Kate and Roger go down to the pool. Kate reads there and does some laps. I stay up in the condo, read a book, and enjoy the nice AC. Per usual it is very humid…about 90%. I decide to have a cold Tiger Beer.

Later on, Kate, Roger and I have an early supper at the Food Court. Another great Asian meal with rice, veggies, etc. for about $5.00. We stroll over to the Mayamar Hotel on Hovendon Street to be sure that the 6 pm Night Safari bus still stops out front. It does.

We buy our bus ticket and safari tickets together ($35.00 in Singaporean money). It takes about forty-five minutes to get to the safari park. It is HUGE! Acres and acres. Loads of people. Disney-like lines but very well organized and the lines move fast. Another example of how efficient the Singaporeans are. State-of-the-art designing: typical Singapore. Over one hundred nocturnal animals. It is now completely dark. We get into our open-air tram with about twenty other people. I have an outside seat. Good.

The tram trail goes through eight geographical regions. Animals come very near the tramcar. One of the first animals we see is a huge lion...not too far away. We journey from the Himalayan foothills to the savannahs of Africa on a forty-minute ride accompanied by a tour guide giving commentary. Very interesting. We see many unusual, rare animals that were near to becoming extinct, such as Pangolins and barking deer.

We get off the tram about halfway through and take the walking Leopard Trail. We round a bend and see two beautiful leopards behind a glass window. A huge leopard lays down right next to the thick glass in front of us. There is only about one inch of glass separating us! We see Fisher Cats, which are about twice the size of a domestic cat. We come to the home of the Malayan Flying Foxes and giant Flying Squirrels. These animals are housed in a giant walk-through, caged dome with jungle trees and flora. You feel like you are really in a jungle.

We walk through three separate entrance gates. We close the last gate and find ourselves inside a huge caged, jungle area. Suddenly, from out of nowhere, a huge flying squirrel soars through the air right at Roger! This thing is really big and looks like a small flying area rug! Roger ducks and the squirrel shoots up in the air and out of sight. This squirrel scared the wits out of all of us. Beautiful and amazing, but so scary.

We leave the squirrel dome and go back onto the Tiger Trail. We walk to the tram stop and continue the second half of our tram tour through the jungle at night. We pass some huge elephants with long tusks. We pass rhinos, hippos and water buffalo. Eventually we come to the end of our ride. What an incredible adventure. Best zoo experience I've ever had. This has been a really good day. Great safari adventure for all of us.

WEDNESDAY, JULY 27, 2013: RETURN TO HOME BASE, LUCKY'S, AND CHINATOWN

We all get up late again. No rush. "Elvira" (the housekeeper) leads us back to Lucky's, the big department store we visited before. This is the place that Kate bought her $3.00 watch which she cannot even adjust already. The woman at Lucky's says she cannot adjust it. She gives Kate another $3.00 watch. Hopefully the thing lasts at least until we get home (USA, that is). We browse around for a bit and then meander back to our condo.

As always, it is VERY humid: 90% humidity again. It is really a good thing that Gail decided against this trip to Southeast Asia during the month of July. When we get back to the condo after lunch, I have a Tiger Beer and some crackers. Kate goes out to the pool with Roger. I read for a bit and then fall asleep. Later we start packing our suitcases. It looks like we have enough room even without the little spare suitcase that I bought for $25.00 in Chinatown.

Kate washes my "whites" in the washer. We all weigh our suitcases and see if we have any other items left to pack. We watch "Law and Order" again on TV, then walk down to the Food Junction (food court) once again. We all have another nutritious meal for about $6.00. Thank God for this food court. We could not afford to eat at a decent restaurant in Singapore. In fact, if it weren't for Roger and his house swap, we would never even have the opportunity to stay in Singapore at all. Thanks, again, Roger! After supper, we take the fifteen minute walk to our high-rise condo. So ends another wonderful day for us all in Singapore.

SATURDAY, JULY 30, 2011: PLANES, PAINS AND MORPHINE

We board our flight right on time, leaving Singapore at 12:30 pm. About three hours out of Singapore, Roger experiences very severe pain in his left side. He got up and lay down in the rear galley area on the floor with some assistance. Knees up. Pain seemed to go away in about fifteen minutes. Roger went back to his seat. Kate was asleep. She wakes up and gives him a sleeping pill. About five hours later, Roger woke up with severe pains again. He went to the rear of plane and lay down again on the floor.

Kate got the airsickness bag out and Roger was sick as soon as he returned to his seat next to Kate. A half hour later he had a glass of water and vomited within five minutes. The flight attendant found two RN's who came over and spoke with Roger. Roger got sick for the third time when we were about an hour-and-a-half from Helsinki, Finland.

He now had to fill out some medical forms in order to get pain medication. At this point, it was around 3 am. There were three "doctors" listed in First Class. So, a flight attendant went and woke them all up to get medical help for Roger. All three said they were PhD's and not MD's. Perhaps they just didn't want to get involved with this situation. Who really knows?

About fifteen minutes later, a nurse gave Roger a shot of morphine in his arm. It takes about half an hour to finally kick in but it does do the trick. Roger's pain level drops from about a nine to a two and the flight attendant tells Kate, Roger and I to remain on the plane when it lands at the Helsinki Airport in Finland.

A few hours later the plane lands. After all the passengers have disembarked, we are called to the front of the aircraft where we have a "conference." The captain is joined by a woman who is some kind of supervisor. There are also three flight attendants in addition to two paramedics with their equipment who board the plane as soon as the other passengers are all off.

All of us gather around Roger as the airline people give us their input. They all agree that Roger should go to the local hospital immediately to get evaluated. They explain that we have a long flight over the Atlantic Ocean and there is no way we can land if Roger has another kidney stone attack. Roger states that he now feels fine and that he would like to continue on to the next stop at Heathrow in London. At this point, the captain informs us that they have already cancelled our reservations to London and that we need to book new reservations so we can continue on to London tomorrow. Meanwhile our luggage is still on the plane booked through to Boston. All we have is a small carry-on each.

Kate, Roger and I have to make some fast decisions. An ambulance with lights flashing has already pulled up on the tarmac outside the plane. It is decided that Kate will ride in the ambulance to the hospital with Roger. I volunteer to go to the terminal and try to get our bags which are stowed and not marked to be taken off the plane at this point. I'm told that a special call was made by somebody and I should be able to pick up our nine bags at the carousel at the baggage claim. As this is being discussed, Roger is escorted off the plane and into the ambulance. He is strapped onto a stretcher inside the ambulance but they are not free to go. They have to wait for immigration to come and stamp some paperwork. Finally, someone comes and stamps their papers and Roger and Kate take off in the ambulance, with a police escort, to the nearest hospital.

At the hospital, Kate and Roger have to wait in the waiting room for about one-and-a-half hours. A doctor finally examines Roger and tells him, "You aren't going anywhere." Roger has an IV inserted and they draw some blood. He is put on a saline drip. While in the waiting room, Roger's pain level was an eight-and-a-half. He is stabilized and his pain level drops. Kate has arranged to meet me at the Kit Kat Café in the airport where I am supposed to be waiting with the nine pieces of luggage. Yup. No stress. All this was easy as pie. Right!

While Kate and Roger are on the way to the hospital, I finally get to the correct baggage claim. I wait and wait for our luggage. Everyone else has since collected their luggage and departed. I speak with the baggage claim lady and she makes a call to check. Finally, the luggage shows up on the carousel. Somehow, I manage to stack up the nine pieces so high I cannot see straight ahead. I have to keep peeking around the corner to see where I am going. Eventually I wend my way to the Kit Kat Café. The plan is for me to stay here until Kate can get out of the hospital and take a cab back to the airport, and, hopefully, locate me and the luggage. We have no cell phones so this complicates things. Like I said: No stress!

Surprisingly, Kate shows up at the Kit Kat Café within two hours. Roger is still back at the hospital. However, he is now feeling better and not in pain. We realize that we will have to stay over this evening and also the following evening. We use the phone at the airport and book a room at a nearby hotel for two overnights. We get more Euros while we are still at the airport. Then we hail a cab and take off for our new hotel.

Once we arrive, Kate and I lug the bags to our room and unpack just the clothes that we will need for the next two days. Then we grab a quick lunch around the corner. I look forward to having a beer and Kate enjoys a nice glass of wine. It has certainly been a busy morning for us all.

After lunch, Kate returns to the hospital to see Roger and I go back to our hotel room. Kate returns with Roger about an hour later. He feels well and looks very good. He is no longer in any pain. The hospital gave him some pills in case he has another kidney stone attack. We call our airline and find out that we will need to stay in Helsinki another full day and night because all the other flights to the USA are booked up. Then our airline calls our room and informs Roger that he will have to fill out two pages of medical forms. The airline tells Roger they will fax the paperwork to our hotel. After Roger fills out his part, the doctor at the hospital must put his signature at the bottom of this form. So Roger returns via cab to the hospital to get the signature. We have a nice supper and go to bed.

SUNDAY, JULY 31, 2011: SINGING IN THE RAIN IN ESTONIA

As Forest Gump so famously said, "Life is like a box of chocolates. You never know what you're gonna get." When we get up today, Kate suggests that we make use of this extra day by taking a boat ride to Estonia, a neighboring Balkan country. No visa or passport is required to enter the country of Estonia. Roger and Kate have already visited this small country but they are aware that I have not been. The ferry ride is only about ninety minutes away. Estonia will now be my seventh country on this amazing adventure (Helsinki, Finland being my sixth). Kate does all the booking online from our hotel lobby. Our boat leaves at noon. The Three Musketeers are off again!

When we get off our the train from Helsinki to the boat port, we don't know exactly which dock our ferry leaves from and we are running a little late. A good Samaritan came to our rescue. He was originally from Texas but he had been living in Estonia for the past twelve years. Thanks to his help and directions we made our ferry just in time. Our Catamaran moved along at about seven knots an hour. After about two hours, we disembarked in the "Old Town" section of Tallinn, Estonia. Tallinn was a charming old city with cobblestone streets and beautiful architecture. We stopped in a cozy old pub for lunch. It reminded me of an English (or Irish) pub. I had beef stew that was excellent.

After lunch, we browsed around the various shops and we each bought an umbrella since it was now raining lightly on and off. With our three bright umbrellas, the three of us looked like we belonged in that old musical *Singing In The Rain*. We stopped again to get

57

something to eat before catching the ferry back to the port in Helsinki. As we ate our food, Nat King Cole was singing, *roasting chestnuts on an open fire*. This was followed by Bing Crosby crooning, *White Christmas*. The date was July 31st. Go figure!

After a leisurely day in Old Town, we boarded the catamaran and returned to Helsinki. When we arrived back at the train station, the ticket window was closed. There was an automatic ticket machine for depositing money and purchasing a ticket. However, this process was very complicated for us and we couldn't understand the language and directions. Almost instantly, another Good Samaritan appeared and volunteered to buy our three tickets for us (and then we could just pay him the money for the tickets). We thanked him and then ran to catch our train back home to the depot.

There were many trains and tracks and it was all very confusing to us. What platform were we supposed to be on? Also, we could not read any of the signs because not one of them was in English. For the third time in one day, we met another good Samaritan. He was a young man in his twenties named David. He came right over to help us and said that he would stay with us on the train since he was going to the same stop in the village where our hotel was. He got off the train with us and pointed us on our way. We were all very impressed with how friendly and helpful all the people that we had met were. We walked the ten minutes from the depot back to our hotel. What a nice unexpected visit to another country!

When we got back to our room, we packed up our suitcases for our return to the US and went to bed early. Another fun, full day.

Good Night, Ma. Good Night, Pa. Good Night, John Boy!

Luckily the rest of the trip home was uneventful. But it was a great experience and is one I encourage others to explore.

****

THE WORLD AS SEEN THROUGH SEYMOUR'S EYES

I am not sure exactly what time it is but I think I overslept somehow. Oh, oh, the digital clock on the bedside table confirms my worst suspicions. It is now 8:46 am. Oh, well, room service is bringing our breakfast at nine. The bellhop is a nice kid and he will be getting a big tip as usual. I must say that this is one of the nicest hotels I've ever stayed at. This room is immense and beautifully decorated. The rugs appear to be Orientals and the furniture and wall hangings are exquisite. But, most importantly, the bed is huge and oh so comfortable. I love the fresh, clean smell of the soft silk sheets.

But, enough, about these creature comforts. I guess it is time for me to introduce myself. My given name is Seymour. My Latin name is Cimex Lectularius. However, I am more commonly known to you as a bed bug. They certainly named me correctly because I do see more of beds than most humans do.

I have heard that some of the young ladies that show up here regularly are called bed bugs too (or perhaps they are just ladies of the evening or high-class escorts). No matter, they are very pretty and everybody has to eke out a living somehow. I have seen many celebs here: the rich, the famous and the infamous. I have seen the best dressers and the best un-dressers for that matter. You folks would not believe the stories that I could regale you with. But I plan on saving those for another time. I want you to know that I am a very high-class bed bug. I reside at a world-famous hotel here in Boston.

I won't go into all the antics that I have witnessed at this fine hotel. Suffice to say I have seen it ALL! When I have more time, I plan to write a complete novel about my experiences here. I plan to entitle it, 'A Bug's Eye View of Boston After Dark'. I can assure you that it will be a very "tit-elating" tale. Ha, Ha! I have to laugh. We bed bugs have a very bawdy sense of humor. How could we not, spending all our time in the sack and observing all the human lusts and foibles as we do?

Now, there is one thing that really does "bug" me, pun intended. I hate it the way we bed bugs have such a bad rep. You human beings actually hate us! Whenever we bed bugs move in, you humans move out ASAP. Talk about prejudice! I see and hear about the Race Card on the wide screen TV. But, what about the Bed Bug Card? Sometimes when people don't want to pay their bill, they go to the front desk and pull out the Bed Bug Card instead of their MasterCard. Furthermore, now I hear that many of these same people are trying to sue the hotels for millions of dollars. But, enough about these devious, cheap, greedy human beings. I am sure there are very kind, responsible humans just as we have our own kind, responsible brethren.

Back to us bed bugs and our lives. We bed bugs have a great life and we want for nothing. Furthermore, we are all world travelers and gad about in the most expensive luggage. Before I moved in here, I was a guest at another luxurious hotel located right on the waterfront here in Bean Town. Right now, I am awaiting my perfect opportunity and then I am hopping in a fancy suitcase and booking it for a real up-scale hotel on Maui.

Hawaii has been on my Bucket List for quite a while. It's easy for me to find out where all our guests are going next because they like to brag and blab out all their plans on their cell phones. Gab, gab, gab! BOR....ING! Also, they love to call all their friends and tell them about how luxurious the hotel is. They ramble on about the view, the room, the room service, and the food ad nauseam. When they start to rave about the king-size comfy bed, I try not to laugh right out loud, because I'm lying right next to them in that comfy bed too! I am even cozier than they are and I'm not paying $500.00 plus a night for the privilege of just laying here. I really wish that I could laugh right out loud. But, alas. I'm just a lowly bed bug and I can't speak up for myself.

I'd like to tell you about a fun trip I had last summer. I flew with Phil Pendergast when he went to Singapore for the month of July on a house swap. During the course of that trip, I visited Singapore, Thailand, Laos, Cambodia, Bali, and Finland . That was quite a trip and I even got to fly on Singapore Airlines, the best airline in the world. I heard Phil say that the flight attendants were absolutely gorgeous. But, alas, I couldn't check them out because I was bouncing around with my buddies in Phil's suitcase that was stowed in the cargo hold. Oh, yes! We bedbugs tend to travel together as one big, happy family. It's almost like a clan. This way we can compare notes about what we see and overhear.

The downside was being cramped in a suitcase for hours and hours.

Phil said that the total flight time alone was twenty-one hours. Imagine how you would feel if you were cramped in with a bunch of clothes in a cold suitcase in a freezing cargo hold for all those hours without any warm, fresh air. It's a good thing that we are so resilient. We can even live for months without feeding!

Anyway, once we finally did arrive in Singapore for the first leg of our vacation, we were in seventh heaven. Once Phil opened his big suitcase, my buds and I hopped right out. Boy, did we ever have a blast in Singapore! We immediately made a beeline for the huge, leather sofa and those nice, cozy beds. We had our choice of five beds! Whoopee! Thankfully the live-in cleaning lady was not very thorough and we were never disturbed. Oh, happy day!

I'll let you folks in on a little secret. Most hotel maids do a lousy job of cleaning and, boy, are we grateful! Now don't go worrying about that the next time you stay at a fine hotel. Just put that thought right out of your mind. Stretch right out and enjoy that bed.

After a week in Singapore, Phil unknowingly took us along on his side trips when he visited Thailand, Laos, Cambodia and Bali. It sure was hot and humid traveling throughout Southeast Asia during the month of July. Phil and his companions were always drinking cold bottled water and wiping their faces with cold face cloths. Fortunately, heat does not bother us bed bugs. In fact, we thrive on it. However, my buddies and I were still glad to get back to our cozy beds that were awaiting us back at the condo in Singapore. Well, I have so much more I'd like to share with you folks. But, you will just have to wait until my steamy bio comes out.

Now don't you be sad that my little story is drawing to a close. There has just been a sudden change in my plans. Now I am on my way to your house! See ya soon!

Your new houseguest,

Seymour

Seymour Butts

A Note of Explanation:

Now perhaps you may be wondering: Just how did I get from Phil's house over to the hotel where I am currently residing? That certainly is a fair question. The answer is Kate (Phil's sister) very nicely transported me and my buddies here. Last week, when Kate stopped over to visit Phil on her way to Costa Rica, she asked if she could borrow his nice, big Luis Vuitton suitcase. Of course, Phil was happy to oblige. Therefore, he grabbed his suitcase that was stored in his attic. However, little did he know that my buds and I were having our own little orgy in there. In fact, there were now many more of us as we are very active sexually. Anyway, Kate packed up the suitcase with as much stuff as she could without going over the fifty pound limit. Then she kissed Phil goodbye and took off for dinner with her friend in Boston. After a nice meal at Maggiano's, Kate checked in here. When she went to open her suitcase to unpack her night clothes and cosmetics, many of us jumped right out on to the bed. So...Voila! That's how I ended up here.

Actually, my extended family is very grateful to Kate and Phil. Little do they realize that they have been very responsible for distributing us to many fine hotels as they travel all over the world. Therefore, we would all like to give them a little shout out of appreciation: "Thanks, guys!"

Hey, remember that old New England adage? "Sleep tight...don't let the bedbugs bite." Ha, ha.

****

POVERTY IN PARADISE

My wife Gail, my sister Kate and I recently returned from a two-month stay in Mazatlan, Mexico. Mazatlan is a city of approximately 600,000 people located on the west coast of Mexico, fifteen miles south of the Tropic of Cancer. Mazatlan is listed among the resort cities of the Mexican Rivera and is referred to as 'The Pearl of the Pacific'. There is also a well-used expression that "Mazatlan is Paradise." There are two main districts in the city. We stayed in Centro, which is the older historic district with many old buildings and monuments. The other district is called The Golden Zone, and that is where most of the large, beachfront hotels and expensive shops dot the coastline.

Prior to visiting Mazatlan, my wife and I had heard about "The Dump Tour" sponsored by The Vineyard Christian Fellowship Church, a non-denominational mission church headquartered in Urbana, Illinois. This church began its mission in 1995 and now twelve Vineyard churches are located throughout Mexico. These churches also serve as "feeding centers" for the extremely needy adults and children, supplying up to 1,000 meals for children on a weekly basis. The dental clinic is open two days per week and charges only twenty Pesos (about $1.40 US) per visit. The church sponsors a scholarship program for poor children. For $125 US per year, a child is provided a uniform, shoes, school supplies and a new backpack; and, their tuition is paid directly to the school. The church also sponsors a Make a Child Smile program that provides new tennis shoes, socks, toothbrushes and toothpaste to over 1,000 poor kids in Mazatlan and the surrounding area.

On Tuesdays and Thursdays the Vineyard Church gathers church members, local volunteers and teams from the US and Canada to go out to the "feeding stations" to bring sandwiches, oranges, cookies and bottles of clean cold water to those children and adults who live in the very destitute colonias (neighborhoods).

The adults at the "dump site" struggle to survive by scrounging through the trash in the slim hope that they can find something to use or sell. Many of these folks use the old tin, cardboard, store signs, tires, rubber hoses and old pieces of wood to construct their humble "houses" that often have dirt floors and no doors or windows. As many as ten people may cram together in these little shacks. These people usually work 12-14 hours per day scrounging through the debris and, maybe, making 100 Pesos (about $7.00 US) for their efforts. The problem is that the maids in the hotels are the first people to sort through the trash. Then the garbage collectors sift through it looking for anything salvageable (saleable). Lastly, these people in the poorest colonias scrounge through the debris again in the hope of finding some item that was overlooked in the first two searches. It is quite sobering to think that these poor folks are living in squalor only twenty minutes from the most luxurious hotels in Mazatlan.

On the first Tuesday of March, my wife, sister and I took a twenty-minute bus ride to the Vineyard Christian Fellowship Church in the Golden Zone. We arrived just at nine and were introduced to a lot of volunteers like ourselves. There were also a few teams from other churches. We were all shown a short film explaining just what the mission of the church was and specifically what we would be doing. It was explained exactly what was to be done at each stop and especially the protocol to be followed when we distributed the food, water, etc.

Next, the supplies were prepared for the "Dump Tour." It was an extremely well-organized process with the women making the ham and cheese sandwiches and packing them with an orange and cookies. The men were in charge of filling and packing the large plastic water bottles. Then the supplies were loaded into two school-type buses and one van. The whole process was streamlined and took very little time. Once all the food was packed in bags, we boarded the buses. There were two bright yellow Mission buses, holding about thirty-four persons each and a yellow van carried about sixteen volunteers.

As we proceeded out beyond the suburbs, it became increasingly dusty and humid. Since this was the dry season there was no greenery at all. A hot, dry dust blew in through the van windows. We passed many areas where some small, modest, cement houses had been built.

64

Then, we continued farther to where the poorest colonias were located. The "houses" were mere shacks made up of boards, cardboard, tin, plastic sheets and old rubber tires tacked together. As described earlier, many had neither windows nor doors. Some had electric power lines looping from one shelter to the next; some had no electric power. Some had a kind of shared water/sewer system, but many appeared not have any facilities at all. I had seen poverty before, but this was the most abject poverty I had ever seen. It was even more moving when I saw how many little children were living in these conditions. Contrary to what many people believe, the people in these areas don't become resistant to germs and infection. Thus many die of illnesses from which we never would.

Before we actually saw the dump, we could smell it. When we did actually see the city dump, it was truly an unforgettable sight. As far as one could see, there were hills of burning debris, smoke, wild dogs, some donkeys and bins and bags of sorted-out materials such as plastic bottles, tires, cardboard, boxes, etc. Amid this scene, scores of people were searching through the trash for anything of some value. Also, despite what some people may have heard, these people are not searching for food at the dump and there were no children there.

When the bright yellow mission buses and van pulled in, it was as if the ice cream man had arrived on a hot summer's day. People dropped what they were doing and scrambled to get to the vehicles. We all took the bags that we had filled and went out among the people to pass out the food and water.

Despite their hunger and thirst, I didn't see any fighting or shoving among the people. The women passed out sandwiches and oranges. The men passed out the large, cold, plastic bottles of water. It was heart-breaking when some people arrived too late to get any food or water. I'm not sure, but I think that there was a stop where those people could get food and water later.

On the return trip, we made several stops at the "feeding centers" where the children were located. When the young kids saw the buses, they ran over and lined up in an orderly manner. There was never any pushing or shoving, etc. Some of the older kids made sure that their younger siblings got a spot in the line. These children were of mixed ages, clean and well-dressed. Some still had on their school uniforms* as school had just gotten out. I was struck by how handsome these children were with their big, brown eyes and broad smiles.

After an hours ride, we arrived back at the Vineyard Church. It was around 3:00 pm and it had been a full day. I had learned a lot and we all had much to reflect on. If anyone would like more information about The Vineyard Christian Fellowship Church, you can visit the church's website at www.mcm.org or E-mail: mzt@yahoo.com.

*A uniform is required to attend any school (public or private) in Mazatlan

A KIDNAPPING AT VILLA SERENA

"Gail, Where's Pepe? I've been looking all over for him."

"I don't know, Phil. I thought he was with you. The last time I saw him was last night when you were walking him down the hall on your way to the bathroom. I think that was about 10:00 o'clock. Don't worry, he's around here someplace. He couldn't have gone too far. Don't forget, the entry gate is always locked, so he couldn't have left the complex. He's probably entertaining someone as usual."

My wife, Gail, and I had been staying in Mazatlan, Mexico at Villa Serena. This was our second winter vacation here and we were renting a nice efficiency apartment in a small complex containing sixteen units. All the units were rented...mostly to retired folks about our age who wanted a warm, sunny place to stay during the cold winter months. Over time, Gail and I had met some really friendly people in this cozy setting located just a few minutes' walk to several beautiful beaches.

I knew all these people pretty well by now since almost everyone here had returned to re-rent their same unit. However, I was now getting really concerned about Pepe. He was such a cute little guy and everyone had really gotten to be quite fond of him. I knocked on several of my neighbor's doors and asked if they had seen him. I went down to the open-air foyer where the round table, chairs and grill were. Not there. I even checked to see if he was floating in the indoor pool. No! Thank God! I had just started up the staircase to check the sun deck where the lounge chairs were, when Gail called me. I could tell by the tone of her voice that she was alarmed.

"Phil, come down to our room right away—it's important!"

I ran down the stairs and hallway to our apartment. Gail was just going inside. I caught up with her and we both entered our apartment together.

"Phil, close the door."

I did. She handed me an envelope. The seal was broken as she had just ripped it open. It was addressed to Felipe and Gail Pendergast. I grabbed the envelope and pulled out a note. It was written on a small sheet of yellow, lined paper.

This is what it said:

Felipe: Don't worry. Be happy.
Pepe the Puppet has gone to a better place.
Relax, more instructions to come!

The note was unsigned. Gail told me that the note had probably been slipped under the door while she was taking a shower. When she first saw the envelope, she thought it was an invitation to go out to dinner with another couple we knew. However, this message was not a cheerful one! Pepe, our beloved puppet, had been kidnapped! But by who? And why? It was a fact the Mexican drug cartels were at war and rival members were turning up decapitated more and more often. In fact, just last week, a bullet-riddled body had washed up on the beach at Stone Island. But an innocent puppet! Why harm a fun-loving little puppet? Perhaps they were holding him for ransom. Gail and I didn't know how may pesos we could scrape together if it ever came to that. The note said "More to come." So at least he was still alive (or in one piece hopefully).

Gail and I decided to use gloves if we handled the note again in case the Mexican police had to dust for fingerprints.

That night at the five o'clock happy hour, Pepe's kidnapping was the whole topic of conversation. Everyone expressed shock and tried their best to console Gail and me. Diane even offered to carry my water bottle the next time we hiked to the lighthouse and Charlie said he would cook us a special filet steak on his grill.

Everyone had an opinion or theory. No one could understand why the kidnappers would want Pepe unless it was for some kind of ransom. But it also seemed unlikely that some drug dealers or cartel members had gotten inside our complex since the outer gate was padlocked 24/7 and we had our own keys. I seriously doubted any of these gentle, loving folks would commit such a dastardly deed. But, again, that gate was locked. Did that mean that the evildoer could even now be in our very midst while we were all gathered here? Was this some kind of scenario out of an Agatha Christie novel like *Ten Little Indians*? Was truth really stranger than fiction? My mind was in turmoil and I knew that Gail and I would have trouble sleeping.

Early the next morning, after a fitful night of tossing and turning, I awoke with a nasty headache. I figured it was caused by angst and stress. However, Gail thought that the most likely cause was the six Coronas I had the night before. Either way, I felt foggy and groggy as I slowly walked down the hallway to the central courtyard. Since it was only 7 am, no one else was there. In another hour or so, many people would be wending their way to sit, read or chat over a cup of coffee. I sat down with my mug of Mexican java and looked over at the indoor pool. I remembered all the happy times we'd had with Pepe as he bobbed up and down on his marionette strings and danced around the edge of the pool with Dilly to amuse the swimmers. As I raised my coffee mug to my lips, I happened to look up and was surprised to see a piece of paper taped to the umbrella pole above the table. I removed the note and saw instantly that it was written on a piece of yellow lined paper like the one I received yesterday. With trembling hands, I unfolded the note and flattened it out on the surface of the table.

This was the new message:
Felipe: You are not taking this seriously. Pepe the Puppet will be harmed if you do not get serious.
We will turn the termites loose on Pepe's stupid head!!
Felipe: Be nice – don't worry!
Unless you continue to act stupid!!
More instructions to follow.

I was stunned and continued to stare at the note before me. It horrified me to think that termites might be turned loose on my Pepe. What a painful, ghastly way to die. What kind of a sadist would resort to such a diabolical thing? Moreover, they had called my Pepe "stupid." Not true! He was certainly no Mensa---but he was no fool either! However, what also bothered me was that the kidnappers thought that I was not taking this seriously. Little did they know that I'd hardly slept at all last night because of this. I got up and walked down the hallway to inform Gail of this latest development.

Early the next morning, after another fitful night's sleep, I poured myself a cup of strong coffee and went down to the courtyard again. Even before I arrived at the table, I was startled by what I saw. There were two puppets on the table along with two short notes. One puppet was quite large with grayish hair. Apparently, she was Pepe's mother. She looked very worried and she had this note clipped onto her:

Where is Pepe? My boy…(Mi Jiho) PLEASE find him!

The other puppet was a very attractive senorita with sparkling blue eyes. She did not have a happy expression on her pretty face. In fact, she looked totally pissed! She had a short note attached to her colorful, Mexican skirt.

The note said:

My name is Lulu. I am
pregnant with the
illegitimate child of
Pepe the Puppet!
Find him NOW!

Oh, no! What else could go wrong! Was this really true? How had Pepe sneaked out and gotten hold of this pretty young thing? I guess he somehow got through the grillwork in the iron gate. Well, I guess true love can overcome many obstacles. Or, perhaps it was purely raw, unbridled lust. Oh, what a letcher little Pepe had apparently turned into! I always knew he had a mind of his own. Now I learned that he also had a libido of his own. Moreover, did this mean that I was about to become a grandfather of sorts? This was too much for me to absorb right now. I'd reflect on that later.

Also, now it appeared that his poor mother was distraught. I had never known much about Pepe's background when I adopted him, but her anguish really registered with me.

I knew that now I'd have to take a more aggressive approach to get Pepe back. But how? If I did receive a ransom demand, I'd do my best to meet it as long as it was reasonable. Maybe I'd have to have money

70

wired from our IRA accounts in the States. If that was the only way, I'd do it. I wouldn't be able to enjoy my retirement anyway if Pepe wasn't around to share it with me.

After a long talk with Gail, we decided that a wanted poster would be a good idea. This way we could spread the word that Pepe was missing. Also, this gesture would put the kidnapper on notice that we were serious and prepared to pay a ransom if necessary. So Julie (an artistic neighbor of ours) made up a nice "wanted" poster and I taped it to the wall in our central courtyard. It seemed to do the trick. Now, whenever friends stopped over, they could let their friends in Mazatlan know that Pepe was missing. Hopefully, this way word would get back to the evildoers if it was not someone already living in our midst.

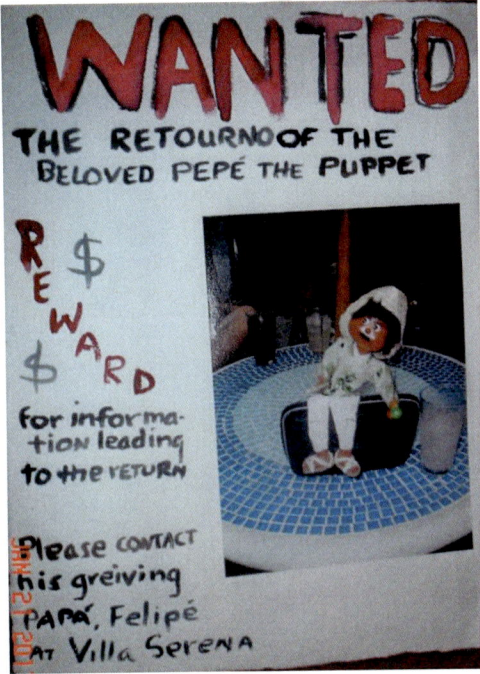

The very next day, the owner of the complex came over with a tech support person to fix our computer system, which was down again. He was not pleased to see our "wanted" poster on the wall. He said we'd just have to put an ad in the Maz newspaper instead. He asked us to remove the poster. Everyone felt we needed to leave it there. So we did.

The following afternoon my neighbor, Dave, came down the hallway and into the courtyard where I was sitting with some friends. He had his hands cupped like he was holding something in them.

"Phil, I found these on the floor in the hallway outside my door this morning." He opened his hands, revealing what appeared to be two toothpicks. "Do you think that this might be part of Pepe? If so, perhaps he is still alive. You know sometimes drug lords send a small body part to the victim's family to ensure that the ransom is paid. At least we didn't find Pepe's little sandaled foot or severed hand."

I agreed that this could be a hopeful sign. "But, Dave, why haven't

71

we received some kind of ransom note?"

"That's true." Dave replied. "It just doesn't make sense. I'm sure if it ever did come down to a ransom request, we could all chip in a few pesos."

I thanked Dave and started to reflect on what the bits of wood could mean.

The next night, I couldn't sleep again. So about 3 am I decided to go out to the courtyard to try to read the paperback I'd brought from home. Before I even got to the table, I was confronted by a most ghastly sight! There was a male puppet strung up by a rope to the top of the umbrella pole! There was a large noose around his neck and his bulging eyes were still open. However, it was plain to see that the poor guy was dead. There was a note attached to the limp body. Again it was written on yellow, lined paper.

This was the newest message:

Felipe:

You missed the 5:00 deadline!
Then you disrespected Pepe's
mother's plea.
So now---we had to hang
Pepe's little brother ---Pee-Pee.
Maybe now you will take us
seriously!!!!
One last chance—shed a tear,
keep a somber face—
don't smile—don't laugh.
Buy some rosary beads and
pray.
More instructions to come!!!!

At this point, I was feeling physically sick. What rational human being could do such a thing to a fun loving little puppet? There was, indeed, a monster on the loose. Perhaps even a serial killer.

I phoned the Mexican police right away. Within minutes, they

72

arrived and taped off the crime scene. We were all told to return to our rooms and stay there until the police could interview us privately. No one was permitted to leave the premises. Even Andrea (the owner's wife) and the tech man couldn't get in! Villa Serena was in lock-down mode. We were all now officially suspects, including the maid, Maria.

The next few days were a blur of activity and chaos. We were all interviewed endlessly. The Mexican CSI was called in. Everyone and everything was searched thoroughly. However, the most intrusive people ended up being the reporters and cameramen. They followed us everywhere! The National Enquirer even tried to get a photo of Pee-Pee in his little coffin!

Since this was the first documented case of a puppet murder, it was now international news. I was even interviewed by Wolf Blitzer on CNN. But, unfortunately, despite all the excellent police work and thorough CSI investigating, the crime remained unsolved. Every lead ended in a dead end (no pun intended).

Often during these days I couldn't help but think of Pepe's mom. First, her oldest son was kidnapped. Next, her youngest son is murdered. What turmoil she must have been in!

Moreover, now Lulu likely presumed that Pepe was probably dead like his little brother Pee-Pee.

But, to me, the most baffling thing of all was this: what was that 5:00 deadline all about? I never received a ransom note.

Who took Pepe ----- and why???

After a few weeks, things settled down somewhat. However, we were all worn out. We all began locking our doors for the first time. We also did our best to "watch our backs." But, we all also tried to help each other get through this ordeal and thus we all became even closer than before.

Finally we started to resume our 5:00 Happy Hours. Dilly cheered us all up with her guitar playing and folk singing. We all missed Pepe, but as they say, "Life must go on."

Then it happened. One very hot afternoon, after a day at the beach, Gail and I returned to our apartment. After we unlocked the door, we almost stepped on an envelope just inside the threshold.

The envelope was addressed to Felipe and Gail Pendergast. I quickly picked it up and tore it open. As usual, the note was written on yellow lined paper.

This was the message:

Felipe:

You can have Pepe back, for free.

No reward wanted. He is not the man puppet we though he was! He must have been carved from bad wood.

He impregnated Lulu and probably many more and caused his brother's death by hanging. Bad hombre!!

Gives a bad name to all Mexican puppets.

Next time do not talk the vendor down ---- pay full retail and get a better product.

Pepe is on the roof (front). He is yours, for free.

You deserve each other.

Wow! I couldn't believe it. Pepe was back! I didn't care what the evildoers said about my Pepe. He was free at last and home where he belonged.

I dropped the note, kissed Gail, and ran down the hallway to the courtyard. I knocked over a chair as I raced by the table where some friends were sitting. I ran up the stairs two at a time to the sun deck on the roof. There was little Pepe lying down on a chaise lounge. His eyes were closed and his strings were tangled up, causing his body to be in an awkward, twisted position.

I gently picked him up, hugged him and started to untangle his strings. As I did this, Pepe opened his eyes and smiled up at me. Tears formed in my eyes as I carefully cradled him in my arms and carried him downstairs to the courtyard.

Gail and some of our friends gathered around and started clapping and cheering. Some even started to weep with joy. Slowly, more and more people began gathering around Pepe, Gail and I until we were lost from view in a sea of smiling faces. Pepe was home at last!!!

To this day, Pepe's kidnapping remains an unsolved crime. Pepe's story even appeared once on "Unsolved Mysteries." Unfortunately, Pepe himself was no help since he was drugged and blindfolded at all times. He'd become so traumatized, he couldn't remember any useful details. Thankfully, Pepe was now back in the arms of his loving Poppa, Felipe. However, it would soon develop that Pepe's travails were far from over.

****

UPDATE:

It just so happened that little Pepe had gotten the wrong senorita pregnant. As fate would have it, Lulu's father was the notorious Carlos "The Knife" Osuna, the most powerful drug lord in the Mexican Sinaloa Cartel. Shortly after his return, Pepe was informed by Carlos that he, Pepe, would end up in splinters if he didn't do the honorable thing. Needless to say, Pepe is now a married man. He now lives in Culiacan with his bride, Lulu, and their little son. Pepe is now very busy working for Carlos running large shipments of drugs along the west coast of Mexico.

Pepe said that if time permits he will try to make a quick visit to Villa Serena to visit his old friends. He hopes to pop in sometime in February while Carlos is away for ten days at the annual drug summit in Medellin, Columbia. Pepe plans to bring along his adorable son, Poo-Poo. In the meantime, he said to toast him with some strong Margaritas during our daily happy hours.

FINITO

SEYMOUR'S MEXICAN ADVENTURE

"Buenos dias, Amigos! It's your old buddy Seymour the bed bug checking in to say, "Hola." I just had to tell you about the wonderful trip my buds and I had to Mazatlan, Mexico last winter. Per usual, we all traveled as a happy little family via Phil's dependable suitcase. I must admit that we have grown to love our little "casa" or "hacienda" in the suitcase lining.

We arrived in Mazatlan on a very hot, sunny afternoon. We all rode in an air-conditioned taxi from the airport to the nice, little apartment that was to be our new winter home for the next two months. What a cozy little abode! Everything was spic-and–span as they say. Nice and clean with brand new bed linens on the big king-size bed. What more could a tired little bedbug hope for? The name of the complex we moved into was called Hacienda Pacifica. Well, I can honestly tell you that after we arrived, that villa didn't stay "pacifica" for long!

Phil and his lovely, unsuspecting wife Gail immediately unpacked their summer clothes and put them in the various bureau drawers. Then they placed their suitcases up on top of the armoire as they always do. As soon as the suitcases were secured and no longer in motion, we decided to have a little "summit meeting" to discuss our vacation plans. We all voted to explore the villa and see just what good ole' Mexico is really like. We had always been curious why more and more "gringos" kept flying down to Mexico every winter. Apparently they didn't care about the drug wars and violence as long as they could sit under their umbrellas, chug their cervasas and sip their Margaritas. Oh well… that is probably why the native Mexicans call the people from the USA and Canada, 'Those crazy gringos.' I suppose because we bedbugs are from the USA we would be considered 'Gringo Bed Bugs.' But, enough about semantics; let me continue with my story.

Needless to say, I for one wanted to check out those Mexican Senorita bedbugs. We had all heard that they were absolutely gorgeous creatures. However, we had also heard from our traveling brethren that most of these young damsels did not speak English. Or, if they did, it was difficult to understand with their accents.

However, I wasn't worried or concerned at all because love (or in my case, lust) can always find a way. Heh, heh. At any rate, we wanted to be sure to get down to the courtyard in time for Happy Hour, which used to commence at five o'clock. Now apparently it can start any time after noon, I've heard.

Well, by the time we crawled to the courtyard, the festivities had already started. There must have been twenty to thirty folks there! Many people sat at the round table and the rest either stood around or brought their own chairs. Everybody seemed to be talking at once as they enjoyed their "adult beverages." I guess these humans call gabbing and gossip "catching up." Whatever, it certainly did appear from a bug's eye view to be a jolly soiree all right. Soon Dilly took out her guitar and led the whole group in a rousing sing-a-long. Man those folks know how to knock 'em back and have a good time. In fact, they were all having such a great time that they didn't even notice the little group of us gathered in the corner near the pool observing all the festivities.

Soon enough we got tired of watching the crazy gringos and we decided that we had to get our clan organized and our sleeping quarters selected. We decided to split up into three cells. Cell 1 would find homes on the first floor. Cell 2 would go to the second floor. Cell 3 would make themselves comfy in the penthouse units on the third floor. I opted to remain with a few of my buddies just where I was in Phil's suitcase lining. We figured that we would use some of these nice folks right here as quick rides to our new homes. We hopped right onto our human "taxis" and they quickly transported us all to our new apartments on all three levels of Hacienda Pacifica.

The very next evening, we made a beeline (or, I should say, "bug" line) to the Plaza Machado around the corner. In the courtyard the previous evening, the gringos were all discussing the various activities that the plaza had to offer. Well, I gotta admit it. Those crazy gringos were right. Let me tell you, we bed bugs all had a blast!

The plaza was really hopping that evening by the time we all arrived (thanks again to our human taxis). I must admit that I for one drank too much of the Tequila that got spilled on one of the restaurant floors. Man is that stuff powerful! No wonder you humans like Margaritas so much. Somehow I managed to crawl out to the sidewalk to check out some of the senorita bed bugs. BINGO! Right away, I spied a most gorgeous gal. Her name was Bonita and boy could she dance! When Rafael Rodriguez played La Bamba, we must have danced for a full fifteen minutes. As I've told you, I tend to fall in love (lust?) fast. Within an hour, Bonita and I were tucked in for the night in my little hacienda in Phil's suitcase. Of course, my buds had also found their own senoritas. So, needless to say a good time was had by all.

As you all know, we bed bugs are very prolific and multiply very rapidly. Soon there were hundreds of us frolicking all over the villa. I had made a pact with my buds that lived with me in Phil's suitcase. It was agreed that none of us would bite or harass Phil or Gail in any way since they were nice enough to treat us all to a two month Mexican vaca in the middle of winter. However, the whole clan was desperate for food sources since our population had increased at a phenomenal rate and now there were a lot more mouths to feed. As a result, very soon our presence became quite evident to all the residents of the villa.

One night during Happy Hour some of my buds and I overheard the following conversation. As Charlie was grilling some steaks on the new grill, he said, "Does anyone else feel itchy and have any bite marks?"

His wife Diane said, "I've been scratching my legs for a few days now. But I haven't seen any ticks or mosquitoes."

Phil commented, "Gee, Gail, and I haven't had any bites or itches."

Then Dilly piped up, "Well, I've been itchy for ten days and I have lots of tiny red bite marks on my back and both of my legs. Hate to say it, folks, but I think we have bedbugs. Here are a couple of the little guys that I found this morning crawling across my mattress." She then unfolded a paper napkin and presented her find to the group.

Once Peter got a look at the little critters, he bluntly commented, "Yup, those are bedbugs alright."

With that, Vania exclaimed, "That's it! I'm outta here unless Conchita gets this place fumigated immediately. It was bad enough last year when we had those giant cockroaches. Remember how we had to have that bug guy keep coming back all the time?"

Conchita, the owner, was called immediately on her cell. Within fifteen minutes, she showed up in the courtyard. I couldn't believe the number of gringos. Almost every person in the complex was present and everybody seemed to be talking at once. A couple of women seemed to actually be hysterical they were so worked up. It was certainly a very emotional meeting and several folks demanded their money back unless we bed bugs were exterminated immediately. Some people wanted to leave on the spot and wanted a full refund. It was utter chaos.

Conchita was very apologetic and promised to have an exterminator come the very next day and spray the entire complex with some kind of powerful gas that was lethal to us bed bugs. All the tenants were told that they had to be out of the villa the next day from ten until five. Everyone was very upset to hear that they had to be away from their units all day and more people threatened to leave. When I heard this conversation going on, I thought to myself, here we go again.

Whenever my buddies and I move in and get comfortable, you humans move right out. Talk about discrimination! But, that's not the worst. Now you want to gas us all! You'd think that we were in a world war or something. Gimme a break!

I immediately hitched a ride on Phil's sandal and made a beeline back to alert as many of my buds as I could. Unfortunately, I didn't have much time. We tried to find as many human taxis as possible to get the word out to the second and third floors.

The next day was a bad one for us Cimex Lectularii. The war started about 10 am and within a matter of hours we had suffered very heavy loses. Hundreds of us lay dying all over the villa. Some of us were wounded and died hours later. The gas odor was horrible and made me sick. However, being off the floor and up in the suitcase, probably saved me and my buddies that terrible day.

Even though that gas attack was very successful, most of the tenants still didn't want to remain at the villa. They claimed that they still itched and were still being bitten. Also, several people had had to go to the local doctor because they had developed infections from their bites. Almost all the gringos found a temporary place to pack in or else they just flew home early. Several people became irate and demanded their money back immediately.

Conchita tried to be fair. She didn't return their money but she did release some of the badly bitten folks from their contracts. As a last resort, she said that she would contact another pest control company and have them place some kind of bombs in the rooms of the few remaining tenants. I couldn't believe my ears. First, they gas us. Now they are going to bomb us! I think all of you humans have gone completely insane. They exterminators did, indeed, bomb the villa and we did lose more of our comrades during that siege. However, the remaining tenants had had enough. The rest of the gringos just threw their clothes in their suitcases and "bugged" out of Hacienda Pacifica. Many of the gringos didn't have much to pack because they had thrown away their "contaminated" clothes. Some folks were so paranoid that they just threw away their suitcases with their clothes in them. Strangely enough, Phil and Gail had no bites or itches and they didn't have to discard their clothing.

After the horror, chaos and confusion of the last few weeks, the villa was now all but deserted. It was like a ghost town. Gone was the sound of laughter and music in the courtyard. No more Happy Hours, just a bunch of empty chairs around the big round table. Even the cats had taken off somewhere. The few remaining folks planned on being out within a day or two. Some Gringos were looking hard for any kind of short-term rental. However, almost everyone went back to the US or Canada.

Due to the extent of their bug bites, allergic reactions, and stress, many people said that they would never set foot on Mexican soil again. It was rumored that Conchita was so fed up with all the confusion, phone calls and loss of income that she was selling the villa. Two real estate agents had been observed walking through the empty hallways just yesterday afternoon. What a different picture from when we first arrived. It was all very sad, indeed.

Phil and Gail decided that they might as well return home also. All their friends had left by now and they really didn't have an alternate place to stay. So, with a heavy heart they decided to fly back three weeks early. It didn't help to know that Boston had suffered a major snowstorm a few days before.

However, despite a nasty war, my immediate family and most of my close buds had survived. This still had been a memorable vaca for me. I had found the love of my life here in Mazatlan.

I married Bonita in the Plaza Machado where we met that first night. Rafael Rodriguez sang the Hawaiian Wedding Song just for us. Bonita is now officially Mrs. Seymour Butts. However, she is commonly known as Bonnie Butts. We are planning on starting our family just as soon as we get settled back in the US. We brought along a few of Bonnie's relatives (she has a big family) and they are teaching me Spanish. I am studying really hard and hope to be fluent very soon.

Well I guess that's it for now. Hasta la vista, Babies!

Tu amigo,

Seymour

Seymour Butts

PS: We bed bugs can go up to a year without feeding, so we're just gonna hibernate up in the attic in Phil's suitcase and wait until he takes us all on a new adventure next year. Sleep tight, don't let the .... you know the rest of it.

MY FIRST AMERICAN CHRISTMAS

The sound of the doorbell woke me up. This time the chimes played "Jingle Bells." The next one would be "Joy to the World." I already knew the rotation. I yawned, stretched and decided to get up.

As I walked out of the bedroom, I was suddenly bombarded with a CD playing loud Christmas music and the sound of many voices. The living room was full of many people dressed in bright holiday clothes. They were all laughing and drinking and having a grand old time for themselves.

I slowly started walking across the living room. However, I was afraid that I might end up trampled by some of the men with those big shoes. I also had to navigate through a forest of women wearing four-inch heels. Those pointed heels looked really sharp to me! No sandals or bare feet were to be found at this soiree. I broke into a run and dashed for the refuge of the kitchen. As I did this, one woman yelled out, "My God, there's a rat!" Then another lady screamed and grabbed her husband's arm.

I ran through the dining room and into the kitchen to escape the pandemonium I had left behind me. I slipped on some water on the kitchen floor and slid under the table where the bar had been set up. A frail looking older lady gasped and dropped her Manhattan. The glass shattered on the ceramic tile floor and the cherry rolled under the refrigerator. Complete chaos ensued. Everybody seemed to be yelling at once.

Finally, Phil came in and reached under the table and picked me up. He gently cradled me in his hands and carried me back into the living room.

"Hey, everyone, I'd like you to meet my little friend Pedro. He's a miniature Chihuahua that Gail and I brought back from Mexico last spring. Isn't he cute?"

Slowly some people gathered around to get a closer look at me. One buxom blonde lady said, "He looks just like a little rat to me. Just look at those bulging, bloodshot eyes. That thing is really UGLY! And, look how he's trembling and shaking. He must be cold or scared."

Well, I wasn't cold or scared at all. I was just totally po'd! I felt like saying, "Look lady with the big hair, smeared lipstick and Tammy Faye eyes----YOU look like Miss Piggy to me." But, of course, I couldn't tell her off because I was just a dog and couldn't speak English, or even Spanish for that matter. I wished that she was the one that was holding me. Then, I could pee all over her. But, I obeyed and sat quietly in Phil's hands and let a few people pet me on my head. It was all very humiliating. Finally, Phil put me down and I ran out of the room as fast as I could. I just wanted to get away from all those weird gringos!

I trotted down the hall in the hopes of getting some peace and quiet. I just wanted to lie down in my own little bed. When I got to my room, the door was closed, so I decided I'd go down to the master bedroom at the end of the hallway. The door was ajar so I went in. The lights were off and the room was quite dark. I was about to lie down on the big queen-size bed but it was piled high with winter coats and jackets. Well, I guess that I will just curl up on the floor in the closet. When I got to the closet, the door was closed but I could hear voices through the louver openings:

"Do you think it's safe here?"

"Oh, don't worry. Nobody is going to be wandering down here. They just put out the food and everyone is in the kitchen or dining room."

"Okay. I guess you're right."

Then I heard the sound of zippers and the rustling of clothes. This was followed by the sounds of moaning and groaning.

"What the heck is going on here?" I thought to myself. "These crazy gringos certainly do things differently than we do in Mexico. Guess I better forget about sleeping in this closet."

On the way out of the bedroom, I noticed that one of the coats had fallen onto the floor. It looked to me to be made of some brown, shiny animal skins.

"I bet that's one of those expensive, mink coats," I thought.

One of the sleeves was open, so I burrowed in and made a little nest for myself. Now I was nice and warm and cozy. Before I drifted off, I thought of how nice it must be in Mexico right now with no cold wet stuff falling from the sky. I dreamed of lying in the sun in the Plaza Machado in Mazatlan. I could hear Raphael Rodriguez strumming his guitar and crooning one of his relaxing, romantic songs. I love siestas:

ZZZZZZZZZZZZZZZZZZZZZZZZZZZZ.

83

Sometime later that evening, I was rudely awakened by Miss Piggy as she stumbled into the bedroom looking for her coat. She grabbed her mink off the floor and shoved her chubby hand into the open sleeve. Boy was I ready for her. I showed her how we do payback Mexican style!

FELIZ NAVIDAD, AMIGOS!

A CHRISTMAS MESSAGE

The Holiday Season is upon us again,
When we pause to remember that special friend.
What shall we purchase as just the right gift
To give that someone a Christmas lift?

Somehow this Christmas just isn't the same,
With so much violence, turmoil and pain.
Many are losing their homes to foreclosure,
And some poor souls will die of exposure.

One day the Dow is up – the next day it's down,
And credit card debt's causing many to drown.
Many men are consumed with their fears,
And some find their solace in too many beers.

We see many large families really in need,
And we're forced to confront our own private greed.
We may feel guilty. We may feel blue.
As we say in frustration, "But, what can I do?"

Yet all is not hopeless. All is not lost.
And much we can do with so little cost.
There are many things to make life worthwhile.
So never underestimate the value of a smile.

Life can be cruel and often unfair.
But oh what a difference when someone does care!
Some lonely teens turn to liquor and drugs,
When often what's missing is our love and our hugs.

Perhaps another's loneliness can be partially healed
When someone delivers them "Meals on Wheels."
And perhaps a relationship we can still mend
When we make that call to an estranged friend.

Of all the gifts that God sends from above,
The greatest by far, is the gift of LOVE.
We can all show that we truly do care,
If with our time and talents, we gladly share.

A BROKEN HEART IN SANTORINI

We were running through the terminal at Charles De Gaulle Airport in Paris. We had just arrived from Boston and only had forty-five minutes to race through the airport and get to the next terminal, which was far away. From there we would board our flight to Athens, Greece. Then we would take a smaller plane to the island of Santorini, which is off the coast of mainland Greece.

It was October of 2005 and my wife Gail, my sister Kate and her friend Roger were going on an eight-day vacation to the island of Santorini. Santorini is one of the Cyclades and is considered by many to be the most beautiful and unspoiled of all the Greek islands.

As I was lugging my roller suitcase up a broken escalator, I had a very frightening experience. Suddenly, I could not breathe! I was unable to suck any air into my lungs. I felt no pain or palpitations at all. However, I definitely felt that I was having a heart attack and that I was about to die.

I cannot even describe how scary this feeling was. This lack of breath lasted for about a minute or so but it seemed much longer. I slumped to the floor and sat there until I was finally able to draw some air. Finally, I decided I would go and try to make our next flight. We just barely made the plane.

We were now off to Athens. After a smooth flight, we arrived during the night. Then we boarded a small plane for the one-hour flight Santorini.

We arrived on the island about 10:00 pm and it was raining very hard. We took a small bus along a winding, mountainous road to the small town of Oia (Wee Ah) where we were staying. When we got off our bus, we were expecting to meet Maria (a friend of the absentee landlord) who was to lead us to our villa. But, there was no Maria!

After finally learning that Maria lived over a hardware store, we were able to locate her. She was a sweet, young girl who spoke but a few words of English. She greeted us wearing a large, black trash bag as a raincoat and led us with a flashlight over a windy, steep trail next to a cliff.

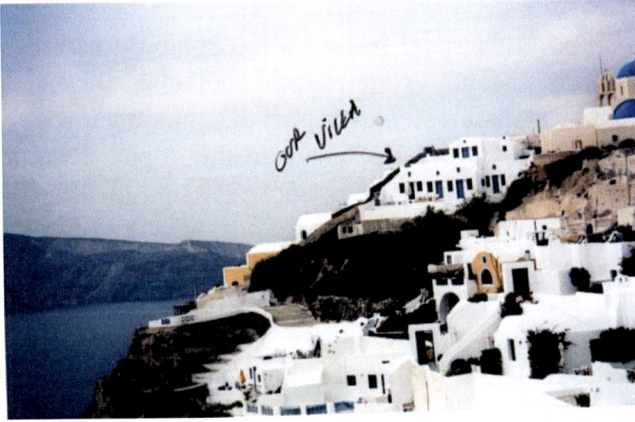

At this point, it was raining very hard and it was difficult to see where we were going. We all had to stop periodically to rest since we were each toting two suitcases.

Finally, we arrived at the villa. Marie unlocked the big oak door and ushered us inside. She explained some things about the villa, gave us the keys and left.

The inside was very spacious. All the walls and stairwells were painted white. All the floors were a beautiful, maroon ceramic tile. The doors and all of the trim were painted a bright blue. It was truly exquisite!

By this time, we were all completely exhausted. We went to our bedrooms and immediately fell into a deep sleep.

The next day, the sun woke us up as it streamed through the large, casement windows.

We walked out to a large, cement patio overlooking the Aegean Sea far below. We were awed to see that our villa had actually been built into the side of a sheer cliff! Far below we could see some cruise ships and, in the distance, the islet of Nea Kamen (the volcano). There is a well-known legend that Santorini is actually located where the Lost City of Atlantis once existed.

Back in the 60s, an oceanographer at the Woods Hole Oceanographic Institution wrote a very compelling book on this subject. It has been well documented that around 1450-1500 BC, the most violent seismic eruption that ever occurred took place. According to Dr. James Mavor, Jr., "The eruption and collapse of Thera (Santorini) was the greatest natural catastrophe that has occurred in historical times." For anyone further interested in this topic, I would recommend reading Dr. Mavor's fascinating book, *Voyage to Atlantis*, © 1969 by James W. Mavor, Jr., G.P. Putnam & Sons, New York, NY.

After breakfast we decided to walk down to the center of Oia and also check out some other parts of the island. Words fail to describe the unspoiled beauty of Santorini. Literally everywhere we looked was a "photo-op." The radiant sunshine reflected off the sea and the shiny blue shutters of the villas. Everything was coated with a white stucco and had a bright blue (Santorini Blue) trim. The white villas almost looked like they had been sprayed with pure white snow.

Later that evening, after dinner, we returned to our villa and went to bed early as we were all tired from yesterday's traveling. Sometime during the night I awoke, not being able to breathe again. I tried to inhale, but nothing happened. Eventually I was able to get some air into my lungs. I now remembered that I had experienced a few cases of sleep apnea at home but nothing like this. I was really scared and really had no idea what was wrong with me. Gail and I slept poorly the rest of that night. We decided to go to the clinic in Fira (the capital) first thing the next morning.

The next day, after breakfast, we took the thirty-minute bus ride to Fira and went directly to the clinic. It was a small cement block building located at the rear of a parking lot. Once we explained the problem, we were ushered into a small emergency room, sectioned off from the hallway by a pull drape. I was placed onto a table and my shirt was quickly removed. They decided to give me an EKG immediately. Twelve rubber three-inch disks were placed on top of my chest. However they were not properly "stuck" onto me. Thus, they frequently fell off and hung next to the table dangling from their rubber hoses. As bad as I felt, this seemed to me to be like a skit from *Saturday Night Live* or maybe even *The Carol Burnett Show* with Harvey Korman as my doctor! This EKG was a far cry from the way we do it in the States with those small metallic circular tapes.

The doctor was a nice man but he spoke no English. He kept saying, "Breathe, breathe!" And, I kept saying, "I am. I am." His assistant was a girl in her thirties who did speak a little English. She did her best to

88

interpret for the doctor. I learned later that she was also a doctor. I asked her if I was having a heart attack. She said, "No. You have an arrhythmia. Also, your heart is beating way too rapidly."

The doctor drew a blood sample and said that he would get the results ASAP. Next he hooked me up to a saline drip bag on a pole. Next a plastic tube was placed in my nose and then connected to an oxygen tank. When I looked at the tank, I was concerned to see that this particular oxygen tank was rusted on the outside. Oh, boy, this sure wasn't looking good.

Now the doctor said I needed to get a chest X-ray to see what my heart looked like. He sent me around the corner and down the hall to the X-ray technician. It appeared that this "technician" was not overly fond of American tourists. She was a big, raw-boned woman with jet-black hair who wore a surly expression in addition to her white lab coat. She basically shoved me up against an antique machine of some kind. It looked like some kind of apparatus left over from the sixties. Or, maybe it was a left over prop from a *Star Wars* movie. Anyway, I was quickly released and sent back to the emergency room.

Next the doctor sent me down another hallway to my hospital room. I had to walk slowly down the hall as I was still attached to my pole on wheels with the saline drip bag and my rusted oxygen tank. My sister, Kate, was at the end of the hallway with her brand new camcorder snapped on and aimed at me. "Are we having fun yet?"

"You betcha, Kate. I'm having a real blast on my second day of vaca on the beautiful island of Santorini."

I continued down the hallway at a snail's pace. Upon entering a small room, I noticed that there were two twin beds. One was occupied. I could see the partial outline of a person with a white sheet and blanket covering the part of the body that I could observe. A bureau prevented me from seeing the top half of the bed. When my wife, Gail, went out to locate a nurse, a disembodied voice from the next bed said, "Are you American?"

I answered in the affirmative and then the voice said, "You don't want to be here. Did you ever see the movie *Midnight Express?*"

I vaguely remembered that the movie had something to do with horrible conditions within a Turkish prison. Hmmmm…

It turned out that the "voice" belonged to a retired sixty-four-year old lawyer from New York named Jerry. He was touring the Greek

89

Islands on a cruise ship with a group of younger travelers. The night before, he'd had a moped accident while riding sans helmet. He skidded on the wet roadway and was thrown off the bike, breaking his collarbone and several ribs. He told me that he had been lying in his bed for over a day and had only been given some water and crackers. Since this was not a hospital per se, they did not provide food for their patients. He was bare-chested and still wearing the same jeans that he had on when he came in. He needed some pain medication and he wanted to leave. However he was in too much pain to move and his ship was leaving the next day. He suggested that I get back to my villa ASAP as there was no point in lying around in this makeshift clinic.

A few minutes later a woman came into the room carrying a syringe of clear liquid. She had no nametag and wore regular clothes. She somewhat reminded me of Cloris Leachman. She told him to turn on his side so that she could administer his shot. He asked what it was but she said, "I don't know." She yanked down his jeans about six inches, gave him his shot and exited quickly. About ten minutes later I asked Jerry, "Are you in less pain now?" He replied that he was not any better and that his pain was actually a little worse.

People came into the room on and off, sometimes speaking Greek, sometimes silent. None of them wore any form of identification. Therefore I never knew if these people were doctors, nurses, CNA's or just the cleaning staff. Once a pretty young girl came into the room and I thought that she was one of the nurses. But she produced a small vacuum, quickly cleaned the floor and then left.

After about one hour of chatting with Jerry, a nurse came in and told me that the doctor wanted to see me again. So I made my way down the hallway yet again, saline drip bag and rusted oxygen tank in tow. As soon as I got to see the doctor he informed me that he had the received the X-rays and blood work back from the lab. He confirmed that I did, indeed, have an arrhythmia but that the x-ray had shown that my heart was not enlarged. However he explained that it was beating way too fast and that he'd give me some medication to slow it down. He next informed me that my triglyceride counts were three-to-four times normal. I was stunned. I thought to myself, I've only been here one day and already I'm told that I have a heart condition and a bad liver. Did this mean I had cirrhosis?

Gail and I asked the doctor what we should do. He suggested flying home or possibly flying back to Athens. Another option was the island of Crete, which was about an hour's flight away.

At this news, Gail said, "But we just got here."

Then the assistant doctor, a female, snapped at Gail, "Well, what's more important, your husband or your vacation?"

Gail had no comment and the silence was deafening.

Gail and I got some digoxin from the doctor. Then we decided to go back to our villa to discuss just what we should do. We took the half hour bus ride back to Oia. I slept well that night and felt much better the next morning. It appeared that the digoxin was working and I could breathe normally. We decided that we would try to continue with our vacation unless I developed trouble breathing again. So we went back to see the doctor to get some more medication. The doctor checked my heart again and informed me that it had slowed down somewhat although I still had the AFIB. He took another blood sample to recheck the triglycerides and told us to come back in a few hours.

We decided to go get some lunch while we were waiting. Before we left, we went to say good-bye to Jerry. We found him just as we had left him the day before. Same bed, same clothes, same position. He was talking with his son who was in college somewhere in the States. After he hung up from his son, he seemed to be in better spirits. However he was still trying to figure out some way to get out of the clinic. He was free to leave at any time but he was in a lot of pain and he really had no place to go. After a while we said our goodbyes and Gail and I went off to lunch. I never saw Jerry again. I often wonder what happened to him. I hope his desiccated remains aren't still lying on that bed.

After lunch, Gail and I returned again to the clinic. The doctor gave me some more medications to slow my heart rate down. He also informed me that my triglyceride counts had gone down somewhat although they were still too high. He suggested that I come back again the next day to recheck the counts. Gail and I decided that we wouldn't come back unless I felt really poorly and had trouble breathing again. So we traveled back to the villa.

I slept well again that night and awoke to the bright sunlight streaming through the large casement windows. We all decided that it would be a great day to tour the island. Therefore we rented a small, compact car and the four of us took off on our adventure.

We drove for about fifteen minutes and soon arrived at one of the famous black sand beaches. We stayed for quite a while and took a long walk on the fine black, volcanic sand. After leaving this beautiful spot, we drove for another hour around the perimeter of the island. Eventually we came to another beautiful beach. This particular beach had fine red sand! We stayed for about an hour and took many photos.

It was now getting to be around noon and we were all hungry. Fortunately, after traveling a few miles, we came to a local winery. The small sign indicated that they served lunch. We toured the winery and had a nice meal outside on the patio with an expansive view of acres and acres of grape vines. We learned that Santorini is well known for its fine wines. Apparently the grapes vines grow very easily because of the rich volcanic soil.

After leaving the winery, we decided to drive to Akroteri, which is a very famous Minoan archeological site with some restored homes featuring beautiful murals, pottery and other artifacts. Akroteri is often compared to Pompeii, although it is not as large or well-preserved. However, when we got to the entrance gate we were saddened to read a sign reading, 'Closed For Repairs.' I was really disappointed, as I had wanted to explore these famous ruins. However maybe it was all for the best. When I returned our rental car, I asked the owner why Akroteri was closed. The man told me (off the record) that a few months ago one of the roofs had collapsed, crushing several tourists to death. So I guess if we had toured Akroteri a few months ago at the wrong time, that could have been our last vacation.

For the remaining days of our vacation, I felt well and had no trouble breathing. Gail and I stopped in Athens for a few days on our return trip back to the States. This side trip had already been booked and the plane reservations had been made in advance. We enjoyed Athens and visited the Acropolis and the Archeological Museum. However, nothing could ever compare to the enchanting beauty of the unspoiled island of Santorini.

Afterward:

Needless to say, I went directly to our local medical center just as soon as I got home. I was given a series of tests including EKGs, a nuclear stress test, X-rays, and echocardiograms among others. As a result of these tests, I was informed that I did have atrial fibrillation or AFIB. Basically, AFIB is an irregular heartbeat caused by an electrical problem within the heart.

Furthermore, I learned that my heart was racing at about 140 beats per minute. As a result, my heart had become enlarged and my heart muscle was weakened. Due to the prolonged rapid rate, my ejection faction (heart output) was very low. I was told with the proper medication and exercise, my heart might heal and get stronger. However, there were no guarantees.

Fortunately, over time, with the help of a great cardiologist, proper medications, prayer and exercise, my heart did repair itself quite well. I will always have AFIB. However, now my heart is normal size, my EF (heart strength) is normal, and I feel well. That fact that I had low cholesterol, low blood pressure and am a non-smoker were a big plus in my ability to recover so well.

Oh, by the way, the doctors retested my triglycerides and all my counts were perfectly normal. So, I was happy to learn I don't have cirrhosis and I can stick to my two glasses of red wine every evening.

OMEGA

LET'S DO A HOUSE SWAP

Over the past twenty years, my wife Gail and I have been very fortunate in being able to go on several house swaps. A house swap occurs when you swap your house, condo or apartment for another place to stay in another state or country. I'm not sure, but I think the concept of trading houses was developed many years ago by some schoolteachers. At any rate, it is very popular now.

The main advantage to the swap is that one gets a free place to stay in a state or country that they have always wanted to visit. There are no agents or brokers involved with a house swap. You deal directly with the other party. There are magazines you can get that have available swaps listed (many times with photos). Also, now with all the hi-tech advancements, a person can do it all on the computer via postings and e-mails. This has sped up the process considerably. Previously one had to write letters or make a lot of long distance phone calls within this country or overseas. Since 1993, thanks to my sister and a good friend of hers, I have been able to go on seven great house swaps. Just to give you a general idea, I will tell you a little about the swaps that I was able to enjoy:

1. Herne Hill, England: 1993

This was my first house swap experience. My sister Kate traded her house on Cape Cod for a second floor row home in Herne Hill, about thirty minutes outside of London. This was a lovely older home. It even came with a car and a cleaner (Wendy).

We were met at Heathrow Airport in London and guided to the house by the owners. They explained things about the house and car to us. They even arranged for us to meet their neighbors next door the following day. We met with the neighbors and we were treated to tea and cucumber sandwiches.

We had a great time and went into London almost every day. It was just a short walk to the local train station. We found that it was about a thirty-minute ride to Victoria Station in London. We were able to see London Bridge, the Crown Jewels, and the Tower where Anne Boleyn was held prior to her execution. We even saw the spot where she was beheaded.

We visited Kew Gardens and drove out to Stratford upon Avon and saw William Shakespeare's house and Anne Hathaway's "cottage." We saw Westminster Abbey, St. Paul's Cathedral, Big Ben, Parliament, 10 Downey Street, and many other places. We had a great time during those two weeks. One thing I didn't get to do was take the Jack the Ripper walking tour at night. The tour goes through the White Chapel area where the bodies were found and ends at the pub that Jack allegedly frequented.

William Shakespeare's Birthplace, Stratford, England

2. Oahu, Hawaii: 1994

Kailua in Oahu, Hawaii is a beautiful place. The house was a ranch style home located on a quiet side street within a short driving distance to most places. The house was immaculate and there was a nice in-ground pool that was very warm since we were visiting in August. The owners also left a newer model car for our use. There was a gardener who came once a week to trim the bushes and shrubs since they grew very fast; we called him Edward Scissorhands after the movie character.

Hanayma Bay, Oahu Hawaii

During our two weeks we got to see most everything on Oahu, including, Waikiki Beach, Diamond Head, the Arizona Memorial (where oil is still leaking after all these years), the Polynesian Cultural Center, Kailua Beach, and many other points of interest. It was sunny every day. If it did rain, it

95

lasted only a few minutes and was followed by a beautiful rainbow! We snorkeled at Hanauma Bay. The odor of the Plumaria flowers seemed to be everywhere.

We left Oahu and flew to Maui for two days. We rented a Mustang convertible and drove on the Hanna Highway (the windiest ride in the world, I think). We drove out to Lahiana, a beautiful fishing village. All in all, it was a memorable, perfect house swap.

3. Galway, Ireland: 1996

We were really happy to visit Ireland since my wife and I have some Irish heritage in our families. We flew directly from Boston to the little airport in Shannon, Ireland. Then we took a taxi to the house that we were to stay in. What a place! We couldn't believe our luck when the cab pulled up to the huge stone Tudor house. In fact, we thought that the driver made a mistake! The house was brand new and set on a nice lot with a long, winding driveway. This swap also included a maid named Eileen who came on "Tursdays" to clean and iron the bed linens and even the towels!

That evening we sat in the living room and enjoyed a glass of wine. As we sipped, we looked around the room. There were open cabinets with all kinds of Waterford crystal glasses and other beautiful items. The rugs and furnishings were exquisite. The owner was a pediatrician at a local hospital. He and his wife had set it up so that we were going for dinner the next night at his associate's house.

When we arrived at the associate doctor's condo. We were greeted at the door by the doctor's wife and shown into the living room. Soon her husband appeared and we all sat down to have a glass of wine. Our hosts introduced us to their three well-mannered

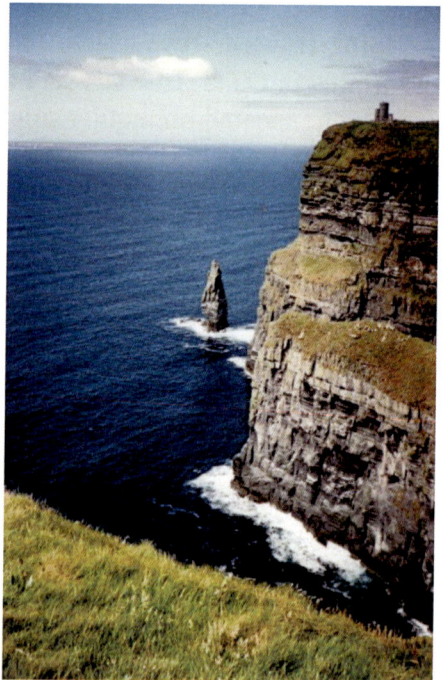

The Cliffs of Moher, Ireland

children. One of the daughters played her violin for us.

Next we sat down at a long table in the dining room for a nice supper. I cannot remember exactly what we had for dinner. However, I do remember that we went through about five bottles of wine! We had before dinner drinks, dinner drinks, after dinner drinks. It seemed that every few minutes our host was popping up to get another bottle of vino.

By the time we left, the sun had long since set on Galway Bay. It was pitch black and the roads were very windy and we had no GPS back then. By some miracle, we managed to wend our way back to our house. I still don't know how we did it without going off the road. It was really late by the time that we all tumbled into bed. It was good that Gail packed some aspirin because the next morning we sure needed them.

During our two-week stay in Galway, we were able to visit many beautiful places of interest. We went to see the Cliffs of Moher (which are about 700 feet high). We also took a tour of the Ring of Kerry and Connemara and took a boat out to see the Aran Islands. Before we left for home, we visited some authentic Irish pubs and toured Bunratty Castle. One day we drove the car out to the town of Killarney and stayed there for a few days. All in all, a truly wonderful house swap.

4. Aix-en-Provence, France: 1997

This was a really super house swap. This time we stayed in a garden-style condo in a beautiful, hilly area of Aix-en-Provence in Southern France. Francois (the absentee owner) left us his Mercedes to drive while we were there. However, there was one little glitch. We had to unlock and detach the steering wheel and bring it inside the condo each night. Apparently this car had been stolen several times. One day we lost the key and had to call "le pere" (the owner's elderly father who spoke no English). We obtained another key so that we could re-attach the steering wheel. But that was a whole story in itself.

After we fixed the steering wheel, we drove out into the countryside. We saw acres and acres of sunflower and lavender fields. Truly beautiful! We continued on to Arles and toured the Roman ruins there. Arles is also where Van Gogh painted several of his famous pictures. He was hospitalized there in a sanatorium for a time. From Arles, we drove to Cannes on the French Riviera and stayed there a few days. The beach was truly beautiful and so were the ladies in their topless bathing suits!

After leaving Cannes, we drove the windy, mountainous road to Monaco. This was the same road where Grace Kelly's car went over the cliff. Beautiful views and hairpin curves. We arrived in Monte Carlo and stayed for two nights in an exquisite older hotel over-looking the marina below. What a view! There was a private yacht there that was supposedly owned by Saddam Hussein's sister; it was gigantic. We never knew if that was really true or not. However, there were armed guards patrolling it with what appeared to be rifles. Later that day we saw the Royal Palace and watched Prince Rainier ride by in his limo with his chauffeur and bodyguards.

The Harbor at Monte Carlo, Monaco

That evening we got dressed up and went to the Grande Casino. That was quite an experience. Since we were not "heavy hitter" gamblers, we were not able to go into the rooms where the crap tables where located. However, we did play the slot machines and I was able to make my forty francs last about forty minutes. It was fun and we enjoyed watching the rich and famous arrive at the front entrance and walk in dressed to the nines. There were some really beautiful Ferraris and Lamborghinis parked out front.

After two days in Monaco, we drove back to the condo in Aix. A few days later, we went to Avignon and visited the Papal Palace and other places of interest. This was one of the most enjoyable house swaps we had ever had. The weather was sunny every day. No mosquitoes or bugs. Every night on the way up the hill to our condo, we stopped at the local market and bought a fresh loaf of bread and a few bottles of French wine. Excellent wine...and about $2.00 US per bottle. I became friends with Martine, the "bread lady", who we saw daily at the "marchee". She spoke just a few words of English. I knew a little French so we were able to communicate all right. After I left Aix, we became pen-pals for a while. I, personally, have always found the French to be very friendly.

PS: One funny aside: One day during a visit to a mall, I needed to use a restroom (not unusual for me). The local facilities were by no means "state of the art." An old lady sat at a beat-up table at the entrance to the two "restrooms." Apparently, one had to pay her in order to use the toilet. When I got up to the table, she said in a heavy French accent:

"Pee pee un Franc. Poo poo deux Franc."

I responded, "Pee, pee." And gave her my coin.

I guess "poo, poo" is more because one is using toilet paper, whatever.

5. San Francisco, CA: 1998

We had a wonderful two-week stay in San Francisco during the month of August. We stayed in a second floor condo in the Castro District, but we didn't have a car to use so we relied on public transportation. During our stay we visited, Fisherman's Wharf, Nob Hill, rode down Lombard Street (the windiest street in the USA), Telegraph Hill and many other points of interest. My sister and I rented bikes in San Francisco and rode them over to Sausalito for lunch.

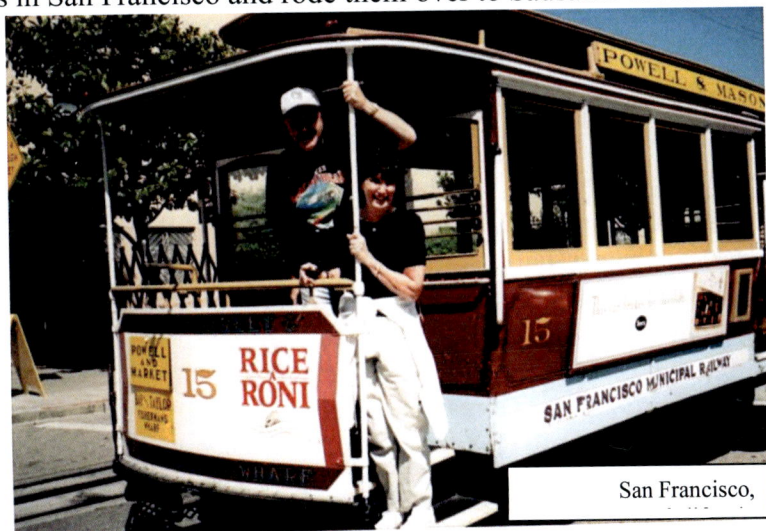

San Francisco,

A few days later, we took the boat out to Alcatraz (The Rock). I learned that Alcatraz Island is now officially a National Park. Using a headset, we took a tour of the old prison. We saw the cell where Al Capone resided. We also saw Richard Stroud's cell; he is better known as 'The Bird Man of Alcatraz'; Burt Lancaster starred in a film about him. During our tour, we saw the three heads that were left on the beds when three inmates attempted to escape. They were not at all realistic looking. It is still being debated as to whether or not the men actually made it. Clint Eastwood starred in a movie about the escape. There was no mention made of Whitey Bulger, although he was also a guest in Alcatraz at one time.

On another day we took a trip to Napa Valley and the wine country. We stopped for a tour and wine tasting at the Mondavi Winery. The next day we visited Monterey, Carmel by the Sea, and Pebble Beach. I thought that Carmel was very over-rated and nowhere near as pretty as many Cape Cod towns. The tour reminded me just how beautiful this New England area is. Perhaps we are spoiled by the quaint small towns and white sandy beaches we take for granted right here. All in all, it was a great house swap and we had great weather the whole time.

NOTE: We found that there were a lot of homeless or displaced people in San Francisco. Many of these people can be quite aggressive. One scruffy character shoved a styrofoam coffee cup in my wife's face and expected some money. When she refused, he became very angry and swore at her. We were told by several shop owners that there is a lot of crime and that one should be very wary of walking around at night.

6. Antwerp, Belgium: 2003

This was a super house swap because we again had a car so we were able to cover a lot of ground and see several countries over the course of our stay. We arrived in Antwerp on a bright sunny day. We were shown into our home by the absentee owner's parents, a very charming older couple. The residence was a stone row home with three floors. There was a long flight of very steep steps to the second floor where my sister's bedroom was located. Gail and I had to go up a steep ladder in order to reach our "loft bedroom" which was basically in the attic. It was so low we couldn't stand up! That wasn't the worst, however. The "bed" consisted of a mattress on the floor supported by some bricks! Gimme a break!

This set up was definitely NOT working for Gail! Or me for that matter. We really did not plan on basically sleeping on the floor in an attic with no light for two weeks. Hmmmm. Sooo...... What to do? Gail and I decided that we would sleep on the second floor in the little kids' bedroom. This meant that we would be sleeping in a bunk bed for two weeks. Well...at least it was better than the floor. Gail took the bottom bunk and I opted for the top bunk. How cool is that?

Later that evening we were invited to have dinner at our owner's parents' home. They were very gracious and we had a wonderful time. They explained a lot about the history of Belgium and Antwerp, in particular.

I was impressed that they spoke five languages. However, I came to learn that is very common since people move quickly from one country to another as we do here from state to state.

The next day we took our car and drove to Amsterdam in the Netherlands. What a beautiful city Amsterdam is! We took a tour of some of the canals and saw many houseboats. We stopped and took a tour of Anne Frank's house; I learned that the family almost made it safely through the war. However, at the last minute, someone turned them in. The father, Otto Frank, was the only one who survived. Interesting but very tragic story.

We visited 'The Headshop' where they sell all kinds of bongs, flasks and other opiate materials since "pot" and other drugs are legal in Amsterdam. There were people on bikes everywhere we looked. Bicycling is the main way to get around in Amsterdam, and bike riders have the right of way. So, pedestrians, you better watch out or you could get clipped. They even have multi-level bicycle garages!

Of course, we had to visit the Red Light District at night. Very interesting. The "ladies" stood in large windows framed by different colored neon lights. They would walk back and forth to attract customers. Some of these girls were really beautiful. Some were not. I guess just about any sexual preference could be satisfied here. You were not allowed to photograph these women. There was a side door where the "Johns" could enter the room behind the window and pay for whatever was on his mind. Prostitution is legal in Amsterdam and well-organized, apparently. These girls are tested regularly and are supposed to all be disease-free and in good health.

A few days later, we drove to Cologne, Germany and stayed at the Dom Hotel. directly across the street from the beautiful Cologne Cathedral. We visited the huge cathedral and did a city tour of Cologne. What an interesting city. We only stayed for one overnight because we had to leave early the next morning to go to Bad Dürkheim, Germany, a lovely wine-growing spa town located at the

Fitz-Ritter Wine Estate (1785), Bad Dürkheim, Germany

edge of the Rhine Plain in the Pfalz region of southwestern Germany.

We had the good fortune to be able to stay for a day and night at the 220-year-old Fitz-Ritter Wine Estate. The reason we got to stay at this gorgeous, active winery is an amusing set of circumstances.

It so happened that the sister of a girl I dated back in my teenage years went to Germany to study German through a program her college offered. She became friendly with the countess that owned this old, family winery. This girl ended up marrying the son of this countess (I think he is considered a baron). At any rate, she married the baron and settled in at the family winery and had four children. She now lives in Germany but comes every summer to Woods Hole on Cape Cod where I grew up.

For over forty years, I never heard anything about my old girlfriend or her sister. Unexpectedly, through a mutual friend, I met this sister in Falmouth, MA. When she learned that I like to travel a lot, she extended an open invitation to drop in to see her if I ever came to Germany. I never dreamed that three years later I would be staying at their guest cottage, sampling their fine wines, and swimming in their pool. I have found that life really is stranger than fiction.

That evening we stayed overnight in the old stone guest cottage on the estate. The sister had organized everything for us. The refrigerator was stocked and labeled with food and many different varieties of their wines including some ice wine that I had never had before. Before we left, Konrad, the owner, gave us a personal tour of his winery including the maze of wine cellars in the basement of the main house. He was very gracious and we had a wonderful time. We had another swim in the pool and then left the estate later that day. We then drove back to the house we were staying at in Antwerp.

While we were in Belgium, we took other side trips and we learned a lot. One of my favorite side trips was to Brugge, Belgium. Brugge is a beautiful, unspoiled old-world city. It was never bombed like many cities during the war. Consequently, Brugge has some of the best-preserved architecture in Europe. When you are in Brugge, you feel like you have actually stepped back in time.

I hope that these short pieces give you a brief idea of what a house swap is like. We have NEVER had a bad or unpleasant house swap. My sister and her friend have always found their homes in excellent condition when they returned home. Nothing was ever damaged or stolen. I hope someone reading this will sometime experience the excitement of a house swap themselves.

****

FAMILY FUN DAY WITH THE BERGERS

It was 11:15 Saturday morning and the Berger household was a whirlwind of activity. Sheila Berger was busy finishing up the cream cheese and olive sandwiches she was preparing. Her husband, Harvey, was just walking in the door after filling the Dodge Caravan with gas. Their ten-year-old son, Hamlet, was upstairs taking a fast shower. Goneril, his twelve-year-old sister, had just gotten dressed and was now putting on her makeup. The dog, Bruiser, had just done a mess on the floor by the back door and he was hiding in an upstairs bedroom closet.

Today was one of Harvey Berger's favorite days of the year. Today was the Berger family's annual Family Fun Day. Every year Harvey would try to come up with a different adventure that they could enjoy together. His goal was to have them all remember taking these family excursions. He called these one-day adventures "Memory Building."

Harvey came from a large, close-knit family. During his growing up years, his dad had always had a special day planned for just the family. Harvey wanted to continue this tradition with his own family. Harvey was a very well-known psychiatrist who specialized in brain cognition and what he coined "imprinting." But Harvey also suffered from OCD and was obsessed about this imprinting of happy family memories in the Berger children's fertile minds.

An hour later found the all the Berger's strapped into their seats in the Caravan, heading off on their new mystery adventure. Harvey never divulged their actual destination until the very last minute. His plan was to create "heightened imagination" to help built up the suspense. Hopefully this technique would help to imprint more indelible memories. Harvey was very successful about imprinting the memories. However these memories were not always happy ones.

After about ten minutes of riding along, Goneril piped up, "Hey, Dad, where are we going this time?"

"Honey, you know I can't tell you. It's a surprise."

"I know, I know. I just hope this Family Fun Day goes better than some of our other ones. Remember that awful balloon ride we took in New Hampshire last year? I was scared to death and I hated every minute of it."

Hamlet added, "Yeah, and everybody in the balloon hated YOU too...after you threw up on two of them. Nobody spoke to any of us for the rest of the ride and we were all trapped up in that bucket thing with your puke and smell for forty-five minutes. Way to go, Gonnereah."

"Well, HAMBerger, remember that wonderful white water rafting trip on the Penobscot River up in Maine? You fell out and ended up stuck under the raft. Everybody thought that you had drowned for sure. Mom and I were crying and screaming our brains out. Then that nice guy dove in the water and yanked you out from under the raft just in time. You were turning blue and threw up all that water. They cancelled the rest of the trip and we all had to return to shore so you could be checked out. Remember how some of the other rafters were pissed?"

"Okay, okay, kids. We have had SOME nice memories. Just concentrate on all the fun times that we have had as a family and stop teasing each other. You know your Mom named you both after those two Shakespearean characters, the melancholy Prince Hamlet and one of King Lear's daughters, Goneril."

"Right, Dad," Ham replied. "But I also remember we took that glider ride down in Plymouth and somehow we ended up landing on Route 3 instead of out in the field like we were supposed to. That was sure a jolly experience. They had to block off all the traffic and the cops had to reroute people and stuff. I remember all the cop cars and blue flashing lights. There was even an ambulance on the side of the road. I was really embarrassed and felt like a complete moron."

Sheila Berger decided it was time for her to try to come to her husband's defense even though she agreed that some of their adventures had been total disasters. However she really loved Harvey and knew that he was just trying to be as good a dad as his own father had been.

"Come on, guys. Give your dad a break. You know how much he loves you. He just wants us to have some great happy family memories like he has. Think positive. Today is going to be a really fun adventure for all of us. I can just feel it."

Somewhere along the way, Harvey had taken a wrong turn and the Bergers were now running about an hour late. Daylight savings had now ended, the sun was going down, and the azure sky was slowly darkening. Harvey wasn't concerned because they were now only minutes away from their secret destination.

All the Berger children knew was that they were out in the middle of nowhere up in the Berkshires. They had been told that any minute their suspense would finally be over. They had turned off the main highway miles ago. Now they were bumping along some back road passing acres and acres of farms and apple orchards. Suddenly they rounded a sharp bend in the road and were confronted with a huge sign in big red letters declaring: KRAZY KAL'S AMAZING CORN MAZE.

"Well, kids, we're here," Harvey proudly announced. "This is the biggest corn maze in the entire USA. I forget the number of acres, but it is humongous. This maze was custom designed by some gardeners from Kew Gardens in England. They worked on the plans for years. Kew even hired special maze gardeners and flew them over here to set this all up. It took a lot of money and time, but the end result was well worth it. This place was even written up in TIME Magazine. What do you guys think? Is this amazing or what? Pun IS intended! Ha, ha."

The Berger siblings were excited now and they both chimed in, "This place looks incredible. I can see why you drove us all the way out here. How long does it take to go through it? How many ways out are there? Where do we go to get tickets and get going?"

Both kids were really enthusiastic now and even Sheila was thinking that this really did look like a lot of fun

Many of the people were heading to their cars now, so the Bergers had no problem finding a parking space. Harvey led the family to the little shed where he purchased their tickets. The ticket man said that they would probably complete the entire maze in about an hour, depending on how good they were. He told them that it took most folks longer than they had anticipated. He also mentioned that they were the last family going through now as it was getting later in the day. He told them to have fun and waved them through the entrance gate. The Berger Family Fun Day had now officially begun.

As the Bergers rounded the first turn in the maze, they were impressed with how detailed the maze cutting actually was. The corn stalks were perfectly shaped and very tall. They were also quite lush and could not be seen through, as had been the case in other mazes they had gone through. It appeared that there had been some topiary figures carved out and placed in the maze. There were carts with pumpkins on them and pieces of farm equipment placed here and there. As they meandered along, Harvey and Sheila were impressed with how realistic the scarecrow figures appeared to be. They actually looked like real people. The attention to detail was truly incredible.

As time wore on, the Bergers moved deeper and deeper into the maze. They could hear other people laughing and joking around in the distance. In the beginning they had passed some other folks wondering through the paths. However, for the past half hour, they had seen no other people. Hamlet had become restless about fifteen minutes earlier and had run off around one of the corners. The Bergers were having a leisurely stroll through the maze and didn't realize just how much time had actually passed.

Sheila checked her watch and was surprised to see that it was now almost 4:30. It was quickly starting to get dark. She began to get uncomfortable and said to her husband, "Harvey, Ham's been gone too long. He should have stayed with us. I hate it when he runs off like that. Now it's starting to get dark and we still have no idea where we are. We haven't even seen a soul for almost an hour. This maze is too complex. They shouldn't have places where you have three choices of what path to take. I'm starting to get cold even with this sweater on. Hamlet Berger! Get back here now! Where are you anyway?"

From a distance, Ham shouted back, "Over here next to the scarecrow with the pitchfork sitting on the hay wagon. You sound far away. Keep yelling and I'll find my way back to you. I'm getting a little cold and I have to go to the bathroom."

Harvey said, "Well, Ham, we must be coming up to some exit soon. I can wait."

The Bergers walked on for another five minutes or so. By then the sun had finally set and it was now full dark. Sheila was now getting anxious and they still couldn't locate Hamlet even though he continued to call out to them.

"Mom, this isn't fun anymore. I'm tired and I want to go home. I'm worried about Ham. Are we finally near the way out?" Goneril asked.

"We're almost there, Honey. Don't worry. I think Ham is just around the corner."

Sheila fished through her pocket book and located a small flashlight that she had almost forgotten about. She clicked it on and they were able to get enough light to see the path in front of them. She dug through her pocketbook again and pulled out her cell phone.

"Harvey, I'm calling 911. I've had enough of this. Admit it.

Everyone is gone and we are hopelessly lost."

"Okay, Hon. I guess you're right. I feel like a real jerk now but go ahead"

Sheila tapped the buttons and made the call. She told the dispatcher her name and that she and her family were lost in Krazy Kal's Corn Maze. Sheila started to give them some more information but the signal suddenly faded and the call went dead. The light on the screen was nonexistent.

"I hope they got the message okay. My phone is out of juice. This could be a long, cold night sleeping next to Mr. Scarecrow. Well, guess we will all have an indelible memory of this Family Fun Day."

Goneril said, "Mom, we're not really staying here all night are we? I just felt something run over my foot. I think it might have been a rat! I wanna go home now!"

"Don't worry kiddo, help is on the way," Harvey assured her.

Suddenly a voice from the cornfield yelled out, "Dad, you've gotta get us all out of here!"

Harvey yelled back, "Hang in there, Ham. Your mother called 911 and help should be on the way now. Keep calling out to us. You sound a lot closer to us now. Mom has her little Mag light with her. She'll keep waving it around. Keep an eye out for a little moving light."

"Okay, Dad. Will do. I'm trying to think positive."

At this point all the Bergers were really starting to get cold. It felt as if the temperature had dropped fifteen degrees in the last hour. Harvey, Sheila, and Goneril walked along briskly in silence, lost in their own thoughts. Sheila was seriously wondering if her message had even gotten through. Then there was the sound of someone tramping through the brush and Ham came flying around the corner with a large old blanket draped around him.

"Mom, Dad. Thank God, I finally found you! That little flashlight really did the trick. I'm so glad you had that. Here, let's wrap this big old blanket around all of us. I figured we needed it more than Mr. Scarecrow."

As Ham was speaking, Harvey thought that he heard the sound of a plane in the background. The noise became louder and louder. Instantly all the Bergers recognized the chopping sounds of helicopter blades overhead. Huge searchlight beams started scanning across the acres of cornfield. Then a powerful search light blinded them all as they stood huddled under their blanket. A loud voice from a bullhorn boomed out to them, "We have located you. We see exactly where you are. Do not move from your position. We have people on their way into the field to get you. We repeat. Stay exactly where you are. There are officers entering the cornfield from two directions right now."

The helicopter continued to circle overhead. At the same time Harvey and Sheila could see some blue flashing lights in the distance. Then more blue lights become visible from a different direction. Now the Bergers could see red and white flashing lights near the blue flashing lights. Harvey wasn't sure, but he thought that the lights might be from an ambulance. Oh, man, he thought. All that is missing is a van from the local news. On second thought, there really could be TV people out there. I really hope I'm wrong about that.

Well, Harvey wasn't wrong. There were indeed reporters and TV cameras from two stations. The Bergers had made the big time! The Berger family was escorted out of Krazy Kal's Amazing Corn Maze by five police officers. There was an ambulance with flashing red and white lights parked across the street with the doors open. Two EMT's walked quickly across the street and up to the Bergers. They were soon enveloped by police officers, EMT's, and a gaggle of reporters. This was one indelible Family Fun Day that they would never forget.

Later on that evening, the Bergers sat in their family room watching themselves on the 11 o'clock news.

After the telecast ended, Harvey clicked the TV off with his remote. The whole family sat there in silence for a few minutes. Even Bruiser seemed to sense that the Bergers were all lost in their private thoughts. He rolled over on the floor, closed his eyes, and pretended to be asleep.

Then Goneril finally broke the silence. "Dad, why can't we just be a normal family like everyone else's?"

"Oh, Honey, don't be sad. There really is no such thing as a 'normal' family. Normal is just a subjective word. For example, The Ozzie and Harriet Nelson family was just a myth. No family really lives that simplistic a life. And 'Leave it to Beaver' was even more unrealistic. Do you think that June Cleaver really wore a party dress, pearls and an apron all the time and danced around her kitchen baking cookies every day? Pure fantasy. Just remember what Grammie Berger used to say."

"I forget. What was that Dad?"

"She said---- 'People are just like a bunch of crayons: some are sharp, some are dull, some are cracked, some are broken, and we come in different colors. But we've all got to learn to get along and live in the same box.'"

"Yeh, Grammie was probably right. From now on, I guess I'll just consider our family a bunch of cracked crayons."

"Good girl, Goneril! That's just how you should look at it!"

****

TERROR BETWEEN THE FLOORS

January didn't even notice it when her Starbuck's coffee cup quivered at the corner of her new mahogany desk. She wasn't even aware when the cup trembled a second time. However, when the whole desk vibrated and the cup fell over and spilled black coffee all over her paperwork, she snapped to attention. Having lived and worked in San Francisco for many years, she had grown used to occasional small shakes and even minor earthquakes. Everyone figured that it was just a matter of time before the Big One hit. But, these days life was charging along at a frantic pace, especially with the rapid increase in the speed of telecommunications. People just didn't have time to dwell on something that had happened way back in 1906.

There was another strong vibration, and this time it felt like the whole office shook. January looked through the large glass window of her new office and saw people scurrying back and forth with their files and laptops. Some people were braced against their desks, holding onto their coffee cups.

Surprisingly, many people did not seem that concerned. This was probably because when the Transamerica Pyramid building was built in 1972, there was much made of the fact that it could even withstand an earthquake. However, for some reason, January felt ill-at-ease. An uncomfortable feeling came over her and she felt the need to leave at once and take her paperwork home with her. She stepped out of her office and mentioned to one of her partners that she was leaving early and would finish her work from her house. She added that she would be in early the following morning for that important phone conference.

January walked briskly down the marbled hallway to the set of elevators at the end. She clutched her valise containing the briefs she had been working on. She smiled and waved as she passed a few young attorneys from a neighboring office. She wasn't even aware when they stared after her as she walked away. In fact, January never seemed to realize just what a 'head-turner' she really was. With her new jade colored business suit and her three-inch Prada heels, she was, indeed, the total package.

January Bray was not just "pretty" or "cute." She was, in fact, a truly gorgeous woman. She was trim, agile and perfectly proportioned. She had shoulder-length reddish-brown hair. Her eyes were a cross between blue and green. People always commented on their unique color. In fact, sometimes people asked her if she were wearing some type of colored contacts. She was frequently told that she looked like a young Rita Hayworth or Maureen O'Hara. Her Aunt Polly had told January many times, "Honey, when the Lord handed out good looks, you came back for a second helping."

January smiled fondly as she thought about Aunt Polly. It had been her Aunt Polly who had actually raised her since January's parents had died in a horrific head-on collision when January was just eight years old. Aunt Polly had been a New England no-nonsense Yankee whose role model had always been Katharine Hepburn.

Aunt Polly had done a fine job of raising January to be a positive, fearless, hard-working woman. January had graduated class president and valedictorian of her high school class. She got a full scholarship to UNH in Dover, NH. She graduated from UNH Magna Cum Laude and then went on to attend law school at Columbia University in New York City. A Fulbright Scholarship paid for most of her expenses at Columbia.

After law school, January was immediately hired by the prestigious law firm of Worthington, Hathaway and Cabot in San Francisco where she now worked. January had risen rapidly up the corporate ladder and was now being considered for a junior partnership. Aunt Polly would certainly be proud of her and how far she had come at the young age of only twenty-eight.

January walked quickly up to the brass elevator door and pressed the round silver button. Within seconds the bell chimed and the elevator door slid open. Just as she stepped inside, there was another violent shake and the building seemed to tremble again. January was starting to feel nauseous and was happy to be vacating this forty-five-story office complex.

Just as the elevator door was almost closed, a man ran up to the door and said, "Wait. Please hold the door." At the same time, he was just able to get his left foot part way in the door.

January pressed the "door open" button and the elevator door rolled open.

A very handsome man quickly entered the elevator. He was wearing a charcoal grey Armani suit, light blue shirt, a bright red Jerry Garcia tie and Gucci loafers. He had carefully styled salt and pepper hair and appeared to be in his late forties. He thanked January for holding the door and flashed her a gleaming smile.

A thought flashed through January's mind: Wow, this guy looks a little like George Clooney. What a hunk!

"Thanks for holding the door for me," the handsome stranger said to her. "I really don't want to be stuck in a skyscraper during an earthquake."

"I totally agree with you," January answered. "I have a bad feeling that this is going to be more than a mere tremor."

"Oh, I think you've got that right," the man replied with another of his bright smiles.

January reached inside her valise and retrieved a copy of the Gazette. At the same time, the man unfolded a copy of the Wall Street Journal that he had been carrying under his arm. January thought that this guy looked like a model for men's magazine as he stood there perusing his paper.

She quickly scanned the top half of the paper. It was all about the latest polls and political news. She unfolded her paper and glanced at the bottom half of the page. There was another article about the serial rapist that had been terrorizing San Francisco for the last six months or more. The rapist had been nicknamed the "Red Rose Rapist" because it was reported that he had a small red rose tattooed just under his left ear. The article went on to state that so far he had raped six women and killed five of them. The latest victim had lived because she managed to pretend that he had successfully strangled her. The scenario was always the same. The man stopped the young women to ask for directions. He was always very calm, polite and soft spoken…"a perfect gentleman." Somehow he managed to pull his victims into an alley or some unlit area between two buildings. He always left a short-stemmed red rose next to the victim. This latest victim had gotten a good look at the rapist. He was very handsome and she noticed the trademark tattoo so she knew for sure who it was. All the victims were attractive young girls with red hair and the rapes all took place in the Nob Hill section of San Francisco where January lived.

The story was continued on page three and January flipped to that page. This time there was a very detailed police sketch of the rapist. He certainly was handsome if this was a good likeness. There was even a separate sketch of the rose tattoo. As January was reading this she suddenly had a very uncomfortable feeling.

This man in the elevator looked a lot like the man in the police sketch. However January just figured that she was on edge because of the tremors and the threat of a serious earthquake. She decided that she would feel a lot better after she got home and had a long bath and a nice glass of Merlot.

Suddenly the stranger in the elevator was standing right next to her, looking over her shoulder. *How had he moved so fast?* She even recognized his cologne. It was the same Polo scent that Todd used. She felt his warm breath on her neck as he said softly, "See anything interesting in the paper, January?"

"No, nothing," she replied. "How do you know my name, anyway?"

"Oh, I know all about you January. I've been stalking you for months. You don't honestly think that you are getting out of this elevator alive, do you?"

As he said this, January took a fast glance at his face. He smiled at her and spoke in a soft, modulated voice. She noted that he had very cold eyes that seemed to bore into her. Furthermore, she was jolted to see that he had applied make up on his skin under his ear. But even with the makeup, she could see the faint outline of a rose.

Just then there was a tremendous jolt and the elevator came to an abrupt stop. At that precise moment, the man clasped his hand over January's mouth and slammed her against the wall of the elevator.

"Don't bother to fight, January. I'm much stronger than you are." In a flash, he grabbed hold of the jacket of her new business suit and pulled hard. The material ripped easily and two of the buttons fell to the floor.

January was a small woman but she was physically fit and actually quite strong. Even though she was just five-feet, two-inches tall, she appeared taller due to her three-inch Prada heels. Most people had no idea that she worked out regularly and had obtained a brown belt in Karate. With a quick motion, she kneed the man as hard as she could in the groin.

The man staggered backwards and snarled at her, "You certainly are a feisty little thing. If I weren't such a gentleman, I would call you a real bitch."

January took advantage of her few seconds and quickly tried to grab at his face and poke at his eyes. However, he dodged quickly and her fingers ended up flattened against the elevator wall. Suddenly there was a very loud booming noise and the lights went out. January tried to reach into her pocket book for the pepper spray she always kept there. But she wasn't fast enough and the man slammed her hard again against the elevator wall. January cried out and crashed to the floor landing hard on her back. When she hit the floor, her pocket book snapped open and most of the contents spilled out onto the floor. She felt around on the floor for the pepper spray but it had rolled away somewhere and she could not find it in the dark. A cold panic surged through her when she realized she had lost her best weapon. Then her hand touched one of the high heels that had fallen off during the fight. She grabbed it tightly in her right hand and tried to get up. In the pitch darkness, she heard the man curse and laugh out loud, "Give it up January; you haven't got a chance."

January wished that some emergency generator would kick in so that she could tell exactly where the man was positioned. But in this blackness, she had lost all sense of her bearings and she had no idea how close he was to her. In the blackness, she couldn't see a thing but she could hear his breathing and what sounded like panting. She wondered if he was in some pain due to her hard kick to his groin. When she finally got to her feet, she felt very dizzy and her back was throbbing in pain. She gripped the high heel even tighter in her hand. Her plan was to gouge him as hard as she could in one of his eyes with the sharp, pointed heel.

Suddenly the emergency generator kicked in. Slowly the elevator was bathed in a dim, yellowish glow. The first thing she saw was the man's face within inches of her own.

His face was contorted in anger and he flashed a sardonic smile as he cooed, "Peek-a-boo, I see you. It's show time and you're on now, January!"

The man quickly shot his hands up and wrapped his strong fingers around her neck. She knew that this was her last chance if she was going to survive. January's adrenaline kicked in and with all the energy she could muster, she slammed the high heel into his face hoping to strike one of his eyes. She missed his eyeball. However, she did make a deep, painful gouge just below his left eye. The man screamed out in pain and cursed loudly. He dropped his hands and held his head with two hands as blood poured from the wound and ran down his cheek onto his light blue shirt.

He backed away from her and pressed one of his palms against his face in an attempt to stop the bleeding. In a voice that sounded like a guttural growl, he said, "Close but no cigar, January. This is it. You are a dead woman."

He reached up again and wrapped two bloody hands around January's slender throat. With almost maniacal strength, he pressed his fingers and thumbs so hard into January's throat that her air supply was cut off and she felt blinding pain, then everything went blank. She slumped slowly to the floor and landed in a pathetic heap with one leg thrust out at a grotesque angle.

The next sensation January felt was a ringing in her ears and the faint sound of voices. She was in excruciating pain and she felt like her throat was burning. She gasped and struggled in an attempt to get some air into her lungs. Her face was against the elevator floor and she couldn't move. She felt certain that her next gasp would be her last.

Slowly January became aware of voices around her. An older gentleman was kneeling on the floor next to her gently rubbing her back. A young man in dungarees, who appeared to be a maintenance man or janitor, stood nearby looking down at her.

January slowly sat up and turned to face the man who was assisting her. The lights were back on and she could see that the elevator door had been partially forced open. They were two feet below the level of the next floor. Somehow, these two men had pried one of the elevator doors open and jumped down into the broken elevator. Her attacker was gone.

"Miss, are you okay? Can you breathe now? Are you in pain? Lean on us and we will get you out of here and get you some medical attention. Do you have any medicine in your pocket book? Your husband said that you are an epileptic and that you just suffered a grand mal seizure. He ran out to locate a doctor and asked us to stay with you until he got back with help."

"That man is not my husband," January managed to whisper. "He's a serial rapist and murderer and he just tried to kill me. He is the Red Rose Rapist who has been killing those young girls on Nob Hill. Please, please, call the police right away. How long has he been gone?"

116

"About ten minutes now," the kindly old man replied.

"You've got to get him," January pleaded. "He's going to get away."

"I'll call security here and the SFPD right now," the janitor said as he reached for his cell phone.

January slowly gathered up the items on the floor that had spilled out of her pocketbook during the fight. As she was putting her shoe on, she noticed some blood on the heel. She carefully removed it again and held it by the toe end. She knew it would be important to preserve any evidence. She asked the janitor to please find a bag to put the shoe in. Then she leaned on the two men and handed them her valise and pocketbook. Very gently and carefully, they lifted her up and out of the elevator. As she was safely placed on the marble floor, she took a quick glance back at the empty elevator. There, in the back corner of the elevator she saw a crumpled red rose with some petals on the floor next to it.

The two men slowly walked January down the corridor to the next available office. They helped her to a chair and the older man handed her a paper cup of cold water from the cooler next to him.

"Let me call the police again for you," he said.

"Okay. But right now, I need to call my boyfriend. He works in the building next door."

While the older gentleman called the police on his cell, January tapped in Todd's number on her ipad. She explained briefly to Todd what had just happened to her. She told him the name of the office she was calling from and what floor it was on. Then, all at once, January started sobbing and couldn't stop. Todd assured her that he would be there in no less than ten minutes.

Todd and the police arrived at exactly the same time. Todd had also called his uncle who was a lieutenant with the SFPD. They all wanted January to go to the hospital right away when they saw her torn jacket and the purple bruises that had formed on her neck. She adamantly refused their requests. However she did agree to ride in the cruiser with Todd to the police station.

When they arrived at the station, Todd sat with January in one of their private rooms. She answered the many questions that they asked her. It seemed that everyone was talking at the same time. That wasn't actually the case, but January was still somewhat in a state of shock, sometimes it took her a few seconds longer than normal to process their questions. They had her sit with a police sketch artist and try to give him the best description she could. The artist could work much faster now since they had the help of state-of-art computer graphics. After January had finished giving her input, they showed her the sketch. The end result was a drawing that very closely resembled the one that they had drawn previously. There was no doubt that this was the same man.

"January, the police want to post an unmarked car diagonally across from your apartment for a few weeks or so. We are all really worried about your safety and are concerned that this man may continue to stalk you. Please go along with us on this," Todd pleaded. He loved January, but he also knew just how stubborn she could be. To everyone's surprise, January said that that would be all right with her. She just asked them to let her know when they were not sitting out front anymore.

She thanked the police officers and the sketch artist and let Todd lead her out of the police station and into his car. January was totally exhausted. It felt like it was ten in the evening instead of only two in the afternoon.

January started to nod off as Todd drove her back to her apartment. When they got there, Todd gently nudged her awake and practically carried her up the front steps of her unit. When they got inside, Todd settled January into her favorite chair. Then he went into the kitchen and returned with two glasses of her favorite Merlot. He sat in the chair next to her and they quietly sipped their drinks. Then Todd got up and put a Josh Groban CD into the Bose player.

They both sat there for a while and enjoyed their wine and Josh's fabulous voice. Eventually January got up and told Todd she was going to take a warm bath before she went to bed. She walked slowly out of the living room and Todd heard the water running in the bathroom. He poured himself another glass of wine and pushed back the La-Z-Boy as far as it would go. He was very worried about January and he kept replaying the day's events in his mind. He hoped that the rapist had been scared off now that there was such an accurate police sketch and that the SFPD was on full alert. However he also knew that when you were dealing with such a psychopathic personality, you never knew just what that person would do.

Eventually January returned to the living room in the new white

Turkish robe Todd had bought her for Christmas. It was one of her favorite things and she wore it all the time. January told Todd that she was so tired she could hardly move and that she was going to bed. Todd sipped the last of his wine, got up and followed her into the bedroom. Todd slipped his clothes off except for his shorts and got into bed with her.

Sometime in the middle of the night, January had a nightmare and started crying in her sleep. Todd encircled her with his arms and held her that way until the next morning.

January bounced back quickly and was even back at her desk the next day. Everyone was amazed that she came into work and they welcomed her back as if she had been gone for weeks. Her boss brought some Starbuck's coffee in for her and somebody went out at lunch hour and brought in one of her favorite salads from the deli next door. Todd called her four times that day to see how she was feeling.

After work he came to her office and told her he had a cab waiting outside so they could go for dinner at her favorite restaurant. January really loved Todd and she felt truly blessed to have this man in her life.

Two weeks later Todd stopped over to play Scrabble as they always did on Wednesday evenings. He also brought over some takeout food from their favorite Chinese restaurant next door. While they were eating, Todd told January that they had taken the unmarked car off duty across the street.

January was actually glad. She didn't even like to remember what she had gone through a few weeks ago. It seemed that that had happened a long time ago. Todd opened up the board and placed it on the living room table as usual. Then he got the bag with the tiles in it and placed it next to the board. He reached in, pulled out a tile and handed the bag to January. When she reached inside the bag she felt something different mixed in with the tiles but wasn't sure what it was. When she withdrew her hand she was holding a perfectly cut two-carat diamond solitaire.

"Oh, Todd, it's beautiful! Does this mean what I think it means?"

"It sure does, Hon. Will you marry me? Or, should I drop down on one knee and ask?"

"Oh, Todd, of course I'll marry you! I'm so happy!"

The next few weeks were a blur of activity. Todd and January both agreed that they didn't want to wait long to have their wedding. They were both low-key people and they both came from small, close-knit families. They decided that they would have a small wedding and get married three months later on July fourth on the beach at a mutual friend's cottage on Cape Cod. All told, there would probably only be thirty to forty guests.

Todd's mom asked if it would be all right if she could have a professional photographer take a picture and put an announcement in the paper. January thought that was a good idea since her mom and Aunt Polly had both passed on and weren't around to attend to those kinds of things.

Later that month Todd came over for their Wednesday night Scrabble game. He asked January what kind of Chinese food she felt like having this time. They decided and ordered, then Todd ran out the door and said that he would be back soon. Todd left quickly and January headed for the kitchen to get some plates for the food. As she was leaving the living room, she noticed Todd's wallet lying on the coffee table next to his baseball cap. Just then her cell rang.

The sudden ring startled her. "Oh, that's Todd," she laughed out loud. "He's got to be the most absent-minded person I've ever met." January grabbed her pocket book and fished out her cell.

"Hello, January," the soft, seductive voice said. "Remember me...your friend in the elevator?" January felt a cold shiver run through her as the honey-toned voice oozed through the phone

"We have some unfinished business to attend to. Oh, by the way; you look so hot in that Kelly green dress. It really accentuates those highlights in your beautiful, red hair. You know how much I admire redheads. You really should draw the drapes when you stand in front of your windows."

"Where are you?" January finally managed to ask him.

"Oh, I've been away on vacation. But I wanted to be sure to be back in time for your wedding. I saw that beautiful engagement photo and notice in the paper. You can count on me to show up for the big party. I wouldn't miss it for the world."

Then there was a click...and just the sound of the dial tone.

FINIS

Author's Note: A special thank you goes to Audrey Damon-Wynne for her suggestion about the use of a Prada high heel.

CALL INTERRUPTED

Shelby Whitney was having a bad day. In fact, she was having one heck of a rotten day. Ever since her feet hit the floor this morning, everything had gone south. First, she discovered that her brand new Toyota Camry had picked up a nail. The left rear tire was as flat as the proverbial pancake. Since her husband Tyler had already left for work, she'd had to call AAA. The guy was very nice and replaced the tire quickly. However, she was still behind schedule since it had been an hour before he was able to make it to her condo.

While waiting for AAA, Shelby got a call on her cell. Her current sale was falling through. Due to a bad home inspection report, her clients were pulling out. Shelby had offered to try to see if she could get some of the problems corrected by the sellers. She had even suggested that, perhaps, she could get a price reduction. However, her buyers told her that now they didn't want the property under any circumstances. This was the second sale she'd lost this month due to a bad home inspection and very nervous first-time buyers. "Man, the hits just keep on coming," she said to herself.

Shelby managed to get to her office just in time for the weekly house tour. This morning they had six houses to preview. Shelby always enjoyed seeing the new listings and she started to feel a little more optimistic now. She was pretty sure that one of her clients would love the last house on the tour. She had already showed them over forty homes and they really wanted to purchase before the rates inched up again. This house had all the bells and whistles and it was just in their price range. She called them on her cell as soon as she got back to her office. They sounded really excited and said that they would like to see it tomorrow after they got off work.

Finally things appeared to be picking up. However Shelby knew that in real estate anything could happen. It was never really over until the commission check was in her hand. Even then, sometimes there were complaints about the purchased property despite the fact that the sale had already closed.

Before Shelby left the office, she checked her messages. Then she called to confirm an appointment with a customer that she was meeting down in Plymouth later that evening. This was going to be a second showing on an older colonial home that Shelby had shown them a few days ago. The listing broker had set up this appointment for seven pm. Shelby didn't mind evening appointments. However, daylight savings was over and it would be after dark now. Shelby was not that familiar with the Plymouth area. Unfortunately, last week her GPS had been stolen so tonight she would have to rely on her maps.

Later that evening Shelby sat in her car in front of the antique colonial home. She checked her watch for the third time in five minutes. It was 7:15. Where were the Baron's anyway? This was really very aggravating. Just then, Shelby's cell rang. It was Margo at the office.

"Shel, it's me, Margo. I have bad news. Mrs. Baron just called and said that they have to cancel. One of their kids was rushed to the hospital. Appendicitis attack or something. Sorry to have to tell you this. Mrs. Baron sounded really upset. Gotta say that she was very apologetic though. Said she'd call you tomorrow."

"Thanks, Margo. I understand. Hope their kid is okay. Gotta go. This has been one long day. I'll be glad to get home and have a nice quiet dinner with Ty."

Shelby went up to the house and let the owners know that the buyers couldn't make it. They were very nice and understanding. Well, that was a small relief. Sometimes, in a case like this, the owners somehow end up blaming the broker.

Shelby returned to her car and headed for home. Today had been one very stressful day and she was totally exhausted. She was looking forward to settling into her recliner with the new quilt that Ty had bought for her last Christmas.

They actually had twin chairs and they liked to discuss their days over a nice glass of wine. Shadow, their cat, would most likely be curled up on Shelby's quilt waiting for her.

Despite her fatigue and the bad day she had experienced, Shelby considered herself a very blessed woman. She had married Tyler, her high school sweetheart, three years ago and they had a happy marriage and they both enjoyed their careers. Their plan was for Shelby to work for a few more years to save more money for the purchase of their first house. Then they would sell their condo and buy a garrison style home with a nice piece of acreage. They hoped to start a family and Shelby would work part-time for her parents at their clothing store.

Since it was now completely dark, Shelby didn't notice it when the first raindrops splattered on her windshield. However, after a few minutes, it seemed like the sky had opened up and it was now raining really hard. This was Shelby's worst driving nightmare. She hated driving at night. But she really dreaded driving at night in the rain. She had good vision but the glare of headlights from oncoming cars really hurt her eyes and caused her to squint in order to read the road signs. She figured that with any luck she should be home in about forty-five minutes.

Shelby was disappointed to see that the rain was not letting up at all. In fact it seemed to be raining even harder now. She knew that her turnoff should be coming up soon and she could finally get off the highway. However, as soon as she was on the exit ramp, she realized that she had turned off too soon and that this was the wrong exit. Oh man, she thought. I just don't believe I did this! Now, I'll have to turn around and get back on the highway.

Shelby continued for a few miles but she didn't see any road signs at all. Then she saw a sign through her blurry windshield: entering Duxbury. Duxbury! Great, I don't believe this. I am now out in the middle of nowhere on some back road. Shelby found that she was on a very dark, winding road. There were no street lights at all and she found it a big strain on her eyes to just keep on the road. She really missed her GPS.

Shelby drove for another two or three miles and she still didn't see any route signs or road signs for that matter. It wasn't raining as hard now, but it was still pitch dark. Shelby hadn't even seen any houses in the last ten minutes. Where the heck was she anyway? Was she still in Duxbury? Was she even heading North anymore? Her eyes were starting to sting and she was getting really tired. She was also starting to feel faint since it was a long time since she'd had lunch. To top it off, now she felt like she needed to go to the bathroom. Boy! This sure had been one beaut of a day. She wished that Ty were driving now or, at least, was here so that she could talk with him. He was very smart and always knew just what to do in any situation. That was one of the big reasons that Shelby had married him. She liked to be able to lean on him and let him make the decisions. Decision making was definitely not her strong suit. She had no desire to be a go-getter career woman.

123

She would be very happy to be just a cookie-making June Cleaver or a soccer mom.

After another two miles on the dark windy road, Shelby started to become really anxious. She decided that she had better let Ty know that she was running late. She grabbed her cell off the console and tapped in the number. After six rings, Ty finally answered.

"Hi, hon. I'm on my way home. Took the wrong exit and I'm on some side road somewhere in Duxbury, I think. Wish you were here… Yeah, you're right…I know. Yup, I will. Oh, don't forget to feed Shadow. The cat food is in the left cabinet under the sink. There should be a brand new…"

Just then Shelby became aware of bright lights bearing down on her from her left. The car just came out of nowhere! Shelby screamed out "Oh, my God! Noooooooooooooooo!"

There was the horrific sound of a loud crash, a brilliant flash…and then nothing.

While she was talking on her cell, Shelby had failed to see the red stop sign and gone right through it.

****

Shelby did have one piece of good luck that horrible day. The accident happened diagonally across the street from an occupied house. The owner immediately called 911 and the local police. The police, ambulance, and paramedics arrived within minutes. Shelby was med-flighted directly to Boston Medical Center. She arrived at the hospital in poor condition. She had sustained multiple injuries including a severe concussion, a broken arm, two broken legs, a partially crushed vertebral column, and a punctured lung. Shelby endured countless surgeries and her doctors considered it a true miracle that she survived. Despite all the heroic efforts and multiple operations, Shelby will be confined to a wheelchair for the rest of her life.

Author's Note: According to the National Safety Council, "28% of traffic accidents involve talking or texting on a cell phone."
The Harvard Center for Risk Analysis states, "The use of cell phones by drivers caused approximately 2600 deaths in 2002." Since then this figure has gone up considerably. It has been estimated that over 250,000,000 Americans now own cell phones.

BREAK OUT

Pixie stood on the front porch and waved goodbye to the Millers. "What a nice young couple," she thought to herself. "This garrison would be the perfect house for them and their two small children, and this quiet dead-end street is a perfect place for them to ride their bikes. Plus, that huge backyard would be great for baseball games and family parties. I can already picture them living here. They seem really interested. I think I'll e-mail them those extra pictures I still have in my camera."

Pixie was smiling as she walked back into the house. This open house had certainly been a big success. She must have had at least eighteen couples go through this afternoon. She was really glad that she had extended the time period for another hour. In that last hour alone five more couples had shown up. Even though it was now four o'clock, she knew that she would still have time make her nephew Josh's soccer game.

Pixie Taylor was a very attractive thirty-two year old woman with bright blue eyes and flaxen blonde hair worn in a shag cut. Her first name was actually Patricia, but her parents and friends never called her Patty. From the time she was a little kid, she was known as Pixie because she had always been smaller than her peers. Even as an adult, she was a mere four feet eleven inches and weighed only ninety-eight pounds. However, despite her small stature, she was quite strong and a bundle of energy. Some of her close friends even called her "Flash" because she never seemed to sit still and was always on the go. Pixie was very athletic and she loved baseball and football. She was also an avid kayaker and rock climber. But the thing that was now taking up most of her time and energy was her job. Pixie loved people and she loved seeing and showing houses. She had definitely found her niche when she settled on real estate as her career. Over the last few years, she had become a very successful and sought after broker.

Pixie walked into the kitchen, picked up her mug of lukewarm coffee and popped it into the microwave to reheat it. Once she heard the familiar ding, she removed the mug and sat down at the kitchen table. She took a few sips of the hot liquid and then started to sort through her paperwork. She picked up some of the extra flyers that were left on table. She scanned through her open house sign-in sheet again. After checking to see how many people had left an e-mail address or phone number, she totaled up the names again. She found that there were actually nineteen clients signed in. The fact that there was now a shortage of available properties and the interest rates were slowing increasing was causing some of the buyers on the sidelines to finally come forward. Just this morning, there had been an article in the Globe pointing out the severe shortage of listings. "Good for the Sellers…Not so good for the Buyers," she thought.

Pixie placed her listings, extra flyers, and sign in sheets inside her new valise and zipped it closed. She decided that she better get moving if she was going to make the game. She walked through the house and checked all the rooms to be sure the lights were all turned off and the windows were closed and locked. She left a short note to her clients to let them know how good the turnout had been. Then she put down the automatic garage door, put on the house alarm system, locked the front door, and pulled it closed.

Pixie started to untie the helium balloons from the lamppost but she changed her mind. She decided to leave them there for the owner's children. She walked across the lawn and down the long driveway and picked up the Open House sign placed near the street. She folded it up, returned to her car and popped open the trunk with the remote. She had just placed the sign in her trunk and was closing the lid when she heard the sound of a car turning into the driveway.

It was an older model Toyota Camry that had seen better days. The car sported a lot of rust and dirt and was crying out to be taken to the nearest car wash. "Oh, great. I hope that this guy is just turning around and not a customer."

A young man about thirty years old, wearing a black sweatshirt, faded Levis, and well-worn sneakers stepped out of the car and said, "Hi, sorry I'm late. My name is Ted Ryan. Is the Open House still on? I saw the sign at the end of the street and the arrows pointing down here."

Pixie hated it when people showed up late like this. She'd already been here over three hours and now she was running late for her favorite nephew's last soccer game of the season.

"My wife and I have been looking for a home in this development

126

for quite a while now. She's still stuck at work and asked me if I would check this house out for her."

Pixie was caught off guard a bit and she wasn't sure exactly what to do. She decided that she would give him her business card and a flyer and show him very quickly through the property.

"Sure, I'll take you through, but it will have to be a quick tour because I'm running a little late for another appointment. If you think it's something your wife would like, I can meet you back here again tomorrow. Come on. Follow me."

As she started walking back up to the house with this man, Pixie had a very uncomfortable feeling come over her. She sensed strongly that there was something really "off" about this guy. She couldn't explain her feeling. But something didn't seem right. He seemed to have a very intense manner about him. Almost antsy. She took a quick glance at his left hand. No ring. Hmmmm. Well, she knew that some men just didn't wear their wedding ring. She had an uncle who was a plumber and he was afraid that his ring might catch on something. Consequently, he didn't wear it anymore.

When she was putting the key into the lock, she turned and got a good look at the man's face close up. Now she felt even more uneasy. There was something about his eyes. There was no sparkle in them. It was as if his eyes were devoid of any emotion at all. All she could think was *he has dead eyes*.

Pixie opened the front door and then held it open. As he walked by, she was sure she smelled alcohol on his breath. She then quickly turned the corner and deactivated the alarm system before this man could peer over her shoulder. She led him through the living room and into the kitchen. She enthusiastically pointed out the cherry cabinets, the center island, and the new Black Diamond granite counter tops.

"This kitchen and the two bathrooms were just remodeled this spring," Pixie told her customer.

"Wow, these countertops are beautiful. They look sort of like mother of pearl. I can see little pieces of blue chips inside the granite. My wife will just love this kitchen and I like the set of sliders leading out to the rear sun deck. Would you show me the master bedroom? It says here in your flyer that it has its own full bath with a whirlpool tub. I think she'd really go for that."

"Sure," Pixie said. "Just follow me."

As they ascended the stairs to the second floor, Pixie made a decision. When they got to the door of the bedroom, she would stand outside and let him walk through the bedroom and bathroom by himself. That way she wouldn't be trapped in the room with him. But Pixie never got that chance. Out of nowhere, a hand with a cloth in it covered up her nose and mouth while his other hand held her head in a vise-like grip. The last thing Pixie remembered was a sickening sweet odor and then she passed out.

****

The first thing Pixie became aware of was the noise. The discordant sounds became louder and louder and she thought that it must be some kind of music. She tried unsuccessfully to open her eyes. Then Pixie realized that they might already be open. Everything was pitch black. She felt dizzy and had a headache. She had never felt this weird in her life. Was she really awake now? Was she dreaming this? Was she, in fact, dead?

Pixie's mind slowly began to clear and she realized with panic exactly where she really was. She tried to move her hands and feet, but she couldn't. They appeared to be tied somehow. Then she tried to yell out. Forget it. Her mouth had been taped shut. At this point, Pixie felt nauseous, was totally terrorized, and she knew exactly what had happened to her. She was stuck in the trunk of her client's beat-up old Camry. The noise she heard was the rap or acid rock coming from a CD or the car radio. Her mind started to race and her whole body began trembling. She prayed she didn't have to vomit because she would not be able to open her mouth.

After a few more minutes, the nausea passed and Pixie was able to think more clearly. She knew her only chance of survival was to somehow get out of this trunk. Pixie started to struggle with her hands. She was a tiny girl and had little wrists. However she had developed very strong hands due to her rock climbing. She felt that there was some give with the cord. She continued to twist and turn her wrists even though it was very painful and the rope cut into her skin. Within ten minutes, she had been able to slip one hand through the rope. Soon after that, she was able to get her other hand out. Maybe the guy had been in such a hurry or so intoxicated that he had not bound her tight enough.

128

The next thing Pixie did was rip the duct tape off her mouth. It burned when she did so but that was certainly a small price to pay. She drew up her legs as close to her stomach as she could and worked feverishly to untie her feet. They were tied very tightly but she was able to finally free them. Next Pixie felt around the trunk to see if there was anything in it to help her break out somehow. She searched around and was able to feel a blanket, coiled rope, a small axe or hatchet, a shovel and a flashlight. She immediately pressed the button and the trunk was filled with light. Now Pixie's sharp mind came into focus as well.

She searched immediately for any type of trunk release tab or pull cord. This was an old Camry and there was none (or it had been broken off). When she rolled backwards again, the blade from the hatchet jabbed into her back. Right away she knew that this was her best weapon and only chance of escaping somehow. Pixie tried to figure out how she could use this unexpected find to her advantage. Suddenly she remembered a true account of how an abducted woman had managed to escape from a car trunk. She had broken out one of the brake lights and managed to push her arm through the opening to attract the attention of another motorist. A driver behind the trapped woman saw the arm protruding from the trunk and immediately called 911 on her cell. The police arrived within minutes and the kidnapped woman was rescued. Pixie knew that this scenario would be her only way to attract attention and that her time was fast running out. At this very instant she could be only minutes from the driver's destination.

Pixie rolled over to the front of the trunk and used the seal beam light to examine the area where the lights must be. She found that there appeared to be a plastic panel covering up the brake light assembly. The bottom of this panel appeared to have dried up somewhat over the years and had started to pull away where the panel met the trunk floor mat. Pixie pulled hard on the bottom. It started to open a little and she could see a bunch of colored wires and the light fixture inside. She knew that the hatchet would break through the plastic easily. However, she didn't know if she could break all the way through the brake light assembly. Without any further thought, Pixie whacked away at the plastic panel cover. With three hard blows of her hatchet, she had a big enough opening to reach her hand in. She pulled as hard as she could with two hands and the plastic panel finally gave way and fell off.

Now Pixie was staring at a maze of different colored wires and the light fixture and some bulbs. She knew that the next part would not be easy. She'd have to really slam that hatchet hard into the assembly to break all the way through to the outside. What if the driver heard her and pulled over? Thankfully, he still had that awful rap music blaring at full volume. In fact, the whole car was vibrating somewhat. Hopefully she could break through with the axe without him hearing anything.

Each time Pixie swung the hatchet, she used both hands and used every bit of strength she could muster. The less whacks, the less noise. Pixie truly hated rap or acid rock or whatever it was called. But today she was grateful for it. She didn't know what time it was since her abductor had removed her Timex. However it was summer so she was sure it was still daylight. She knew that she was on a highway because every once in a while the driver would meander over onto the rumble strip and there was a loud noise and vibration. Maybe he was driving drunk and would get pulled over by the state police.

After five more powerful axe blows, Pixie broke through! The hole was small but she could see daylight. She shoved her hand through the jagged opening. She could feel that she was cut and she knew that she was bleeding. Then, with an extra rush of adrenaline, she pushed really hard and her arm went through up to her elbow. She was well aware that she had been badly cut from the broken glass, plastic and jagged metal. The pain was excruciating but Pixie was just grateful to have broken through. She waved her harm back and forth frantically in hopes that a driver riding directly behind her or passing her would notice and call the police. After about ten minutes, she heard the sounds of police sirens. She was sure that help was on the way. However, the sounds grew dim and faded away. She figured that the police cars were on some side road paralleling the highway.

Pixie was now feeling very faint because she was tired and losing blood due to her badly cut arm and hand. Then she heard the sounds of sirens again. This time they were very loud and she knew that they were near the car. She felt the car slow down, pull over and come to a stop. She could hear the sounds of loud voices and a man yelling and cursing. A minute later the trunk lid popped open and Pixie was almost blinded by the bright sunlight.

Two state troopers leaned into the trunk and gently started to help disengage her arm from the jagged brake light hole.

"Are you all right, Miss? We just got the 911 call from the man traveling behind you.

"I'm okay, officers. It's just that my arm really hurts."

"Don't you worry; we are taking you right to the hospital. You were very clever to break that hole through the light. This guy is a serial killer who is wanted in three states. We consider you a very brave young lady."

The two officers helped Pixie out of the trunk and walked her over to one of the police cruisers. She noticed that there were three cruisers pulled over to the side of the road with all their blue lights flashing. The police car with her abductor in it was visible down the highway, speeding to the state police barracks with lights flashing and siren blaring.

****

Author's Note: This short story is a work of fiction. However there have been cases where abductees have been rescued from car trunks by using the tactic employed here by Pixie Taylor.

MY LAST PASSING

It was a sunny June morning and I was in great spirits. I was retiring after thirty-two years of selling real estate full-time and today was going to be my last passing (or closing). For anyone who may not know, a passing refers to the procedure where the final papers are signed when a property is sold. The buyers and sellers sit down at a table with the broker(s) and the bank's attorney. There are always a lot of papers that must be signed, including the mortgage note, the deed, disclosure forms, settlement statements and many more. These various papers are passed around the table for people to sign. Thus the term "paper passing." These passings are usually happy events and tend to take approximately thirty minutes to an hour, depending upon the number of papers to be signed and the efficiency of the lawyers.

I did have one closing where the sellers were divorced and accompanied to the passing with their own attorneys. They refused to sit in the same room so the paperwork had to shuffle back and forth between two rooms and two extra lawyers. That was a long passing and not at all jolly! Thankfully, that is not a common occurrence. At the end of most passings, everyone usually shakes hands and walks away happy. That is what I envisioned for today.

I had made arrangements to pick up my seller at her house and give her a ride to the passing and back home again. I arrived at the house at the appointed time and was greeted by my client, Mrs. X, and a friend of hers. I found the house was totally empty and had been well-cleaned. Mrs. X was just putting the last carton in the trunk of her car. She was in good spirits and ready to go.

It was a bittersweet day for her as she had spent many happy years in this house with her husband up until the time he passed away a few years earlier. Also, during the last week or so, Mrs. X had been tired and mentioned that she hadn't been feeling well. I assumed that this was probably because a happy chapter in her life was now officially ending. Just before we left, Mrs. X's friend pulled me aside and told me that Mrs. X was not still not feeling well and suggested I keep a careful eye on her. I said that I would and returned to my car to drive my client to the passing.

After driving along for about ten minutes, Mrs. X asked me to pull over. She said that she was feeling faint and needed to get out of the car and "get some air." I quickly pulled over as much as I could, but there was a curb and no way to get totally off the road. Mrs. X got out and proceeded to walk back and forth by the side of the road. I got out of the car to walk with her. This probably lasted about ten minutes or so and I really couldn't tell how she was feeling. She didn't want to talk. She just paced back and forth. A couple of times a few cars bombed by us at a good clip. They were only a few feet from where we were standing. I thought to myself, "If we don't get back in the car and out of here, this really will be my last passing." A few minutes later Mrs. X said she felt better and was ready to proceed to the lawyer's office.

Despite our little road stop, we arrived at the lawyer's office on time. When we got there, we were greeted by the bank's attorney,

We met Mrs. X's attorney, the selling broker, and the young couple who were buying the property. We sat down at the table and the papers proceeded to fly back and forth per usual. Everybody signed where they were supposed to and the passing was coming to a conclusion.

After all the papers were signed, Mrs. X. was given her proceeds check. I was disappointed to see that this was not a Bank or Cashier's Check. She was going to need to give this check to the conveying attorney when she went to pass on her new home. I was sure that no attorney was going to accept a personal check for this kind of money. This should have been attended to before by her attorney who was still sitting at the table with us.

Anyway, a call was made to the other law office and, of course, they would not accept a personal check from the buyers made out to Mrs. X. I offered to drive Mrs. X over to the bank where the check was drawn. Once we got there we planned on having a certified check drawn so Mrs. X could go on to close later that day on her new home.

Mrs. X didn't completely understand why we had to go to the bank, so I explained what the procedure was. I told her that I would help her with whatever she had to do. She was very appreciative and got back in my car. After we had only gone about ten minutes, Mrs. X said, "Stop the car. I feel really sick. I have to get some air."

I pulled right over and Mrs. X again got out of the car and walked around by the side of the road. This time I was able to pull off onto a soft shoulder so we weren't in danger of getting picked off.

Mrs. X did not get sick. Good. About ten minutes later we were back "on the road again" as Willie Nelson likes to sing.

When we got to the bank, I walked into the lobby with Mrs. X. We met with a young woman who was a customer service representative. I explained the situation to the young girl. She made some calls. There was apparently now some new problem because Mrs. X was not a member of the bank. I told the girl that I didn't understand why there was a problem since the check she was holding was drawn from their bank and there was more than enough money to cover it. She said she had to make some calls to supervisors or Donald Trump, or somebody. Oh, Brother! Meanwhile, Mrs. X was getting upset and really feeling sick now. She wanted to go outside "for some air" again. I excused myself and escorted Mrs. X. over to my car. During the last few hours the temperature had gone up quite a bit, even though it was early June. I walked around with Mrs. X for a few minutes. Then I put her in the car and turned the air conditioning on. She said that made her feel less sick. I told her I'd be right back.

Back inside the bank the customer service rep told me that they could issue a Bank or Certified Check once Mrs. X signed some paperwork and became a member. I was told to get Mrs. X and have her come back in and sign the forms, then they would issue the check. I went back outside to my car to check on Mrs. X and hopefully bring her back inside the bank to sign the forms and finally get her check. Mrs. X was feeling better but she said she was still tired. Well, I sure didn't blame her. I was feeling sick and tired myself. A simple paper passing ended up turning into a major ordeal. And it wasn't over yet. Mrs. X still had to pass later this same day on her new home.

Finally, the cashier's check was issued and Mrs. X and I were on our way back to her house. Before we had even gone a mile, my cell phone rang. It was Mrs. X's attorney. He wanted to know if Mrs. X was able to get her new check. I answered that her check was now in her hands. He responded that that was good news and now Mrs. X could pass at four o'clock today on her new house. I assumed he was going to be at the second passing but I really didn't know for sure since I wasn't involved in that part of her transactions. He asked to speak with her. He did briefly and then she hung up. About five minutes later, my cell rang again (unusual for me). It was the office manager of the park that Mrs. X was moving to. Her mobile home was empty and ready. The previous people had moved out on time. There was a van with all Mrs. X's furniture and belongings parked next to her new home. The office had the keys. Only one more detail: I needed to get right down to the lending institution in West Bridgewater ASAP and pick up another check that Mrs. X needed to fully pay for her new home.

What? I didn't know anything about this. I was not involved with this part. Mrs. X had bought directly from the Mobile Home Park and she was represented by her own attorney. Now I had to rush down to West Bridgewater before the bank closed so that Mrs. X could get her second check. Apparently, the place was closing within a matter of minutes. I thought, "Man, I do not believe this!"

At this point, I honestly cannot remember the exact sequence of events since it was seven years ago. I know I got down to the lending institution on time. I cannot remember the details now but there was a problem about having to hold her check overnight for some reason. Honestly, I don't remember the exact problem. The long and the short of it was the mobile home park would not let Mrs. X move in until the next morning. The sellers had cleaned the unit, moved out, and signed their papers. However the mobile home park wouldn't let Mrs. X move in until her check had time to clear or someone signed off. Whatever, the problem, Mrs. X was homeless. The young couple was moving into her house right this minute! I had to admit that this was particular problem was a first for me. Did Mrs. X have any family or relatives in this area? What about some really close personal friends with an extra bedroom for one night? Nope and nope. "Houston, we have a problem."

I felt bad that Mrs. X had no place to stay overnight. I was sure she didn't want to stay in a hotel or motel. She seemed really weak and now she was beginning to get very anxious. Moreover, I had a feeling money was a little tight and she wasn't really prepared to shell out an unexpected $100.00. Suddenly I had the solution to her problem. I asked Mrs. X if she would like to spend the night at our house. Then I would take her to the mobile home park the next morning so she could pass on her new home. She was very surprised but she sounded receptive.

"But, won't your wife be upset to have a total stranger as a last minute house guest?"

"Oh, don't worry. My wife, Gail, is a very understanding person and we have two guest bedrooms."

"Well, that certainly is very kind of you. I really had no idea what I was going to do and I'm starting to feel really sick right now. I'd just like to lay down for a bit. Do you live around here?"

"Ten minutes away. Do you feel well enough to ride in the car that long?"

She said that she thought that she would be all right riding for a while longer. I told her we would be at my house within minutes and that she could lie down right away and rest.

Shortly, we arrived at my house. Mrs. X was very weak and just wanted a glass of water and a nice bed to lie down on. I got her the water and led her to my son's old bedroom. She lay down and was asleep within minutes. As soon as I walked into our living room, my cell phone rang. It was my wife Gail asking where I was. She was in a restaurant in the next town waiting for me. We had arranged to meet another couple there for pizza as we often do on Friday nights. In the confusion of the day, I had forgotten that it was already 5:30. She was a little aggravated and told me to hurry up and get over there as soon as I could. I was already late and they had to order. The place was really busy as usual. I told her there had been a little glitch.

"What do you mean a 'little glitch'?" Gail asked.

I explained about the passing and the problems with the check and that this poor woman had no place to go.

"So, where is this little old lady now?"

"She's sleeping in Jason's old room."

"You must be kidding?"

"No, no really. She's exhausted and feeling sick to her stomach."

"Look, Phil. Go and see if she's okay. Maybe she needs a doctor. Maybe there is something seriously wrong with her. What if she dies in Jason's bed in our house? I don't believe you did this! Go right now and check on her. I can't get home for about an hour and a half. Call me after you check on her. Gotta go. The waitress is here again and we have a get our order in. I'll bring you home a pizza. What kind do you want? Do you want me to bring home something for your lady friend? Our friends here aren't going to believe this story. On second thought, I'm sure they will."

I checked our new houseguest again and she seemed fine. She was fast asleep and I didn't want to wake her up. I called Gail again and told her not to worry. All was well and under control. About fifteen minutes later Mrs. X came walking into the living room and said that she was feeling a lot better. Since it was around dinnertime, I asked her if she was hungry. She replied that she hadn't had much breakfast and some soup might be nice if I had any. We went into the kitchen and she sat down at the breakfast counter. I rummaged through our pantry and came up with a can of chicken soup, dumped the contents into a bowl, put it in the microwave and set the timer.

"Dear, I think you are supposed to add some water to that," Mrs. X reminded me.

"Oh, yeah, I guess you're right. I forgot. I'll put a can of water in. No problem."

I added the water and reset the timer. I always have a glass of wine this time of day. Today had been a long day and I was ready. I asked Mrs. X if she would like to join me with a glass of wine. To my surprise, she said "Yes." I asked her if she preferred red or white and she said red would be nice.

Well, that did the trick. She really liked it. So the two of us sat there and sipped our drinks for a few minutes.

My cell phone rang again. I figured that it was Gail calling to see how things were going. Wrong. It was Mrs. X's attorney. He wanted to know if Mrs. X was settled in her new home, etc. I explained that she couldn't move in until tomorrow. He then asked, "Well, where is she now?" I explained that she was sitting here with me having a drink.

"What? Is she all right? What's she doing over at your house? Where is she going to spend the night?"

I explained that everything was under control and that Mrs. X had had some supper and was in very good spirits...in fact...excellent spirits! I told him that she was going to spend the night here. Tomorrow Gail and I would drive her to the mobile home park in my car. We would see that she got settled in. The lawyer seemed somewhat amazed about these developments. However he was happy his client was in good hands. He spoke with her briefly on my cell and then she hung up.

Mrs. X and I returned to the living room and I settled her in a nice comfy chair.

I sat in my La-Z-Boy and put the seat back.

Mrs. X felt great. "What about, perhaps, another touch of wine dear?"

"Sure, no problem. I'll be right back." I returned with the "touch" and we started to watch the evening news on TV.

Soon there was the sound of voices at the front door. Gail and our friends had just returned with a couple of pizzas that were still hot.

I introduced Mrs. X to my wife and friends. Gail served us all pizza and we ate and had a great evening with lively conversation. Two hours later, our friends left. Mrs. X was starting to feel really tired again. It had certainly been a very long, full day for her. Gail got Mrs. X. some towels and toilet articles, etc. Then Mrs. X. went to bed and quickly fell into a deep sleep.

The next morning we all got up around seven o'clock. I was happy to see that Mrs. X looked very rested and she was in fine spirits. Gail made us all a nice breakfast. Then I drove Mrs. X to her old house to pick up her car, which was still at the edge of her driveway. I drove Mrs. X down to the mobile home park and Gail followed us in Mrs. X's vehicle. The park manager met us at the door of her office. She was very helpful and efficient. Mrs. X's friend was also there as she lived in the same park. It was time for us to say goodbye. Mrs. X hugged Gail and she thanked us several times for our kindness to her. She said that she would contact us after she got settled. And so...my last real estate passing had at last come to a close.

****

Author's Note:
Mrs. X called us the next day to let us know that she was happily settled in. She thanked us again and said she'd stay in contact. That Thanksgiving Mrs. X sent us a beautiful flower centerpiece for the dining room table. Every Christmas we receive a nice card and note from her.

CARPÉ DIEM

Carpé Diem---Seize the day!
That's what Horace and the Romans used to say.
It was true then.
And it's still true today.

Life's not a dress rehearsal---It's the real thing.
So hurry up, get going! It's time to act and sing.
Don't worry if you stumble, even if you fall.
Better to have tried and failed - than never tried at all.

Tempus fuget. Time flies. Virgil was so right.
For when you turn around, today's far out of sight.
Time is the fourth dimension, many like to say.
Well, no matter what you call it, we only have today.

Woulda, coulda, shoulda - That's what you always say.
I'll do it all tomorrow for that's another day.
But what if tomorrow you have no second chance,
And find yourself looking back with a rueful glance?

I watch the sands of time slip through my hourglass.
Even as you read this now - That moment's in your past!
So, my friend, Carpé Diem. Run and seize this day.
Grasp it with both hands! Don't let it slip away!

PARTING THOUGHTS FROM SEYMOUR

As I was lying here in my cozy suitcase lining, I experienced a couple of "brainstorms" as you humans like to say. Often times my best ideas come to me early in the A.M. before I even have my first Bloody Mary. At any rate, this is what occurred to me:

1. Why is it that we Bed Bugs don't have our own national (or even international) holiday? After all, every February second, you humans celebrate Groundhog Day and make a big deal about Punxsutawney Phil and whether or not he sees his stupid shadow. Who the heck really cares anyway? Half the time, Phil ends up being wrong. It is high time we Bed Bugs had our own holiday...National Bed Bug Day! After all, there are millions and millions more of us than there are groundhogs. I ask you humans to give this matter some serious thought.

2. Secondly, have you noticed how articles about Bed Bugs are more and more prevalent now? Well, as I've told you----we Bed Bugs are extremely fertile and prolific. You might even say that we have a sex addiction like a lot of your esteemed politicians. By the way...Did you know that we male Bed Bugs have a penis? Yup, it's true! Well, at least we don't photo copy it and e-mail copies all over the internet. Well, anyway, there's no danger of any of us Bed Bugs going into any rehab unless we are having one of our blood drives and we are in desperate need of hosts.

3. But, I digress. I saw recently on Phil's big screen TV that Boston has a serious Bed Bug problem. This mass infestation is taking place not just in the slums but also in some of the most luxurious hotels. But I've already told you all about that. Did you know that the city of Boston is high on the list as one of the ten most infested cities in the whole U.S. of A? Wow! What great PR for all of us Cimax Lectularii. I believe that Boston should henceforth be known as BUG TOWN! It's high time to shake off that old passé nickname of Bean Town. Do I hear any "Ayes" out there?

Lastly…my steamy autobiography, *A Bug's Eye View of Boston After Dark*, is scheduled for release the end of this November. I've made special arrangements with my publishers to have an advanced copy mailed directly to each member of the South Shore Writer's Club, absolutely free as a gift from yours truly. My autobiography would make a super Christmas gift to give to your family and friends. Be aware though that this is an uncensored edition and definitely not appropriate for young readers. Well, I guess that's about it.

Ta Ta…for now.

Seymour

ACKNOWLEDGEMENTS

First and foremost, I would like to thank my wonderful editor Stephanie Blackman for her time, patience and suggestions.

Also, a word of thanks goes to the South Shore Writer's Club for their encouragement, support, and kind critiquing over the last five years.

A special thanks to my long-time, loyal friend Connie Sheridan who introduced me to the writers' club.

Last, but by no means least, a very special note of appreciation to my loving wife Gail, who had to listen to these stories many times as I wrote and rewrote them for this book.

"Muchas gracias a mi esposa."

＊＊＊＊＊＊＊＊＊＊＊